BROKEN

BROKEN

Alyxandra Harvey-Fitzhenry

VANCOUVER LONDON

Distribution and representation in Canada by
Publishers Group Canada • www.pgcbooks.ca

Distribution and representation in the UK by
Turnaround • www.turnaround-uk.com

Published simultaneously in Canada and the UK in 2008
Released in the US in 2009

Mixed Sources
www.fsc.org Cert no. SW-COC-001271
© 1996 Forest Stewardship Council
FSC

The text has been printed on 100% ancient-forest-friendly paper
(100% post-consumer recycled, processed chlorine and acid free)
using vegetable-based inks.

Printed in Canada   10 9 8 7 6 5 4 3 2 1

Cataloguing-in-Publication Data for this book
is available from The British Library.

Library and Archives Canada Cataloguing in Publication

Harvey-Fitzhenry, Alyxandra, 1974-
Broken / Alyxandra Harvey-Fitzhenry.

ISBN 978-1-896580-41-8

I. Title.

PS8615.A766B76 2008   jC813'.6   C2008-902851-1

The publisher acknowledges the support of the Canada Council for the Arts.

 Canada Council **Conseil des Arts**
for the Arts **du Canada**

The publisher also wishes to thank the Government of British Columbia for the financial support it has extended through the book publishing tax credit program and the British Columbia Arts Council.

BRITISH COLUMBIA
ARTS COUNCIL
Supported by the Province of British Columbia

The publisher also acknowledges the financial support of the Government of Canada through the Book Publishing Industry Development Program (BPIDP) and the Association for the Export of Canadian Books (AECB) for our publishing activities.

Sometimes my life is like a fairy tale.

It's not Prince Charming or dancing pumpkins though. It's more like the Grimms' fairy tales. You know, before they were all cleaned up and bleached for proper Victorian children. My story is more like the dark woods and blood falling from fingertips and toes hacked off for glass slippers that don't fit.

Here's the thing.

I'm a freak.

And no, it has nothing to do with my purple hair or nose ring. I wish it were that simple. I can deal with people thinking I'm a freak because of the way I look. That's normal stuff. Maybe not fun, but not that big a deal either. I mean, there are always going to be mean girls in the dark forests of high school. You just have to deal with them.

But dealing with this isn't so easy.

Because how do you explain the way glass breaks around me for no good reason?

CHAPTER 1

Some things are sacred. Like chocolate, Johnny Depp movies…and a girl's bedroom. I mean, seriously. It was bad enough when I got home from school and found the furniture moved around. But worse, much worse, was finding *people* in my room. I froze in the doorway and stared at Ella, my dad's fiancée, and her daughter Katie.

Katie swung open my closet door and shuddered.

"Mom, she like, wears rags. It's mortifying."

My mouth hung open.

"Excuse me! What are you doing in my room?"

Ella and Katie turned toward me.

"Oh, hello, Ash." Ella smiled. "How was school?"

"*What* are you doing in my room?" I marched in and shut the closet door with the toe of my shoe.

Julia, Ella's other daughter, was standing in the bathroom that connected my room to the guest room. She smiled weakly, looking embarrassed. She was annoyingly perfect on a regular basis.

"Your father invited us for dinner," Ella replied.

"In my *room*?"

"No, of course not," Ella said.

I plucked the blue glass paperweight my mom had made for me out of Katie's hand. "Give me that," I said.

"I was only looking at it," she sulked. She was twelve years old and a brat.

"Your father wanted us to come and get a feel of the house before we move in," Ella explained. "He wants us to feel at home."

My father had proposed to Ella last night. I used to like Ella when she was Dad's girlfriend, but now she and her daughters would be moving in. Just before my sixteenth birthday. Some birthday present!

The paperweight in my hand cracked down the centre and I jumped. I looked up, but no one seemed to have noticed.

I just stood there, my heart beating madly, staring at the crack. It looked like ice breaking up on a river. My mother's paperweight. I wanted to cry. I slid it into my pocket the same way I hid the pieces of the cup that broke in my hand last night after my dad announced the engagement.

What the hell was wrong with me? It's one thing to drop stuff. It's another thing entirely when stuff shatters just because you're in the room. I'd broken glass a couple of times since my mom died. And now it had happened twice since the engagement—and the engagement was only a day old. It made me nervous.

"We just need to measure your room so we can figure out where to put Katie's bed. Then we'll get out of your way."

"Excuse me?" I swear my blood went cold, like a river in January. If I were a tree, I would have lost all my leaves right then and there.

"I want to sleep there, under the window," Katie said, pointing to where my bed was tucked under the windowsill.

"That's where I sleep!"

"The guest room will be Julia's," Ella continued, as she pulled a tape measure out of her purse. "You and Katie will share this room."

"Are you kidding? I'm not sharing my room."

"There are only two bedrooms, Ash," Ella said calmly. "Two of you have to share."

"Not *me*!" And *hello*? I bet if she came home one day and I was in *her* room moving *her* bed and going through *her* closet she wouldn't be too thrilled.

I crossed my arms. "Look, no offence, but I'm going to be sixteen next week. I'm not sharing my room with a twelve-year-old." That was *not* what I had in mind for a birthday present. I was thinking more along the lines of a television for my room.

Katie leaped up and glared at me. "It's *my* birthday this week. And I'm going to be thirteen," she said. "And my boobs are already bigger than yours."

Ella looked liked she was trying not to laugh. "I suppose Julia and Katie could share the guest room," she said slowly, as if she was thinking out loud.

"Mom," Julia said, "you promised I wouldn't have to share once I turned sixteen. And I'm already seventeen."

"I'm not sharing," I repeated, just to be sure.

"Oh, girls." Ella pinched the bridge of her nose.

Julia sighed.

"It's okay, Mom. Never mind. I'll share with Katie. It's no big deal."

"Are you sure?" Ella asked, clearly relieved.

"I'll be at university next year anyway."

"Thanks, honey. You're such a good girl." Ella hugged Julia and then tweaked Katie's braid. "Let's give Ash her privacy."

I had barely shut the door behind them when the phone rang. It was my best friend, Mouse.

"You'll never believe what just happened," I said, not even bothering with hello.

"Never mind that," Mouse broke in. "What are you doing before school tomorrow? Because I have a great idea."

"Oh, God."

If the day didn't end in detention, I would be very surprised.

"Pssst."

I jumped and looked into the shadowy bushes.

"I said: Pssst."

I rolled my eyes at Mouse.

"I heard you, weirdo. What are you doing in there?"

She grabbed my hand and pulled me down next to her under the lilac bush. A branch nearly poked me in the eye.

"We have to wait until the janitor's on the second floor."

"It's too early to go all commando," I complained. I couldn't believe she'd managed to drag my butt out to school at this hour for another one of her pranks. I could barely keep track of them at this point.

"No whining." Mouse nudged me. "We're the revolution; show a little enthusiasm."

I just stared at her as if she'd gone crazy. "I don't *do* perky."

She smiled. "You can be the quiet loner with the

blueprints for the building in your pocket next to several fake passports and aliases. I'll be the loud-mouthed activist who creates the distraction."

I had to laugh. "You're whacked. Where do you come up with this stuff? And by the way, you're scaring me. You told me we were going in there to paint on the walls, not break into the principal's office or set the bio lab snakes free."

"Those are both really good ideas."

"Forget it. I like my little misdemeanours. I'm not into serving hard time, unlike *some* people."

Sparrows lifted out of a nearby tree, blurring across the dawn like water bugs over the skin of a lake. One lost its way and swooped down, darting in front of me. A stray feather drifted past my nose. The lights in the second floor classrooms flickered on, and Mouse jumped to her feet.

"Come on." She hefted a large bag, which rattled alarmingly, over her shoulder. "Just paint supplies," she said, taking us around the side of the school. "The moment of truth," she added. "He usually comes in through these doors and leaves them unlocked."

"Who does?" I peered into the bushes, half-expecting a teacher to spring out of the scraggly yews.

"The janitor." She said it like it was common knowledge.

"Okay, seriously, doesn't it creep you out that you know the janitor's morning habits? Don't you think that's a sign?"

"Stop whining," Mouse said, pushing the door open. "Ha! We're in."

I glanced behind us. The streetlights were still on, their light as soft as honey. The clouds gathering in the west looked medieval, like pewter goblets and tarnished swords.

"Come quick, Perrault."

"Yeah, yeah."

We walked down the empty hallways, our shadows stretching over the worn tiles. The school smelled like pine cleaner and bubblegum. Posters everywhere announced that the Halloween costume dance was fast approaching. At the staircase leading up to the bio lab was a mural of historical figures: Shakespeare, Louis Riel, Pierre Trudeau and Champlain.

Mouse stopped in front of it, planting her hands firmly on her hips. Her smile was dark and mischievous.

"This isn't going to be like that fur ad in the bus shelter, is it?" I asked. "I never really got the red paint off my boots."

Mouse pursed her lips. "There's not a single woman in this mural," she said. "They're all dead white guys." She handed me her sketches. "It's ridiculous and wrong and it's teaching us that women have nothing to offer. And that only men are important."

I held up my hand. She was working herself up into another rant. "I got it. You don't have to convert me." I tilted my head. "Out of curiosity, did you ever think of just asking if you could do this? They probably would have given you permission."

Mouse brushed her hair off her face. "You don't ask for permission to challenge the status quo, Perrault."

"I forget sometimes how much you love detention."

Mouse pulled a pencil out of her bag and began to draw on the white wall around the mural. Her hands were quick as wasps. I'd known her long enough to recognize the face forming under her clever fingers. I rolled my eyes at her.

"Not Anne Boleyn again," I muttered.

Mouse grinned. She was infatuated with the Tudor queen whose head was chopped off. We worked quickly. Anne Boleyn and Marie Curie were joined by Charlotte Brontë and Hatshepsut.

I couldn't believe I was just painting away, when my dad was about to get married again. I wondered what my mother would have thought about all of this. I'm sure she would have wanted my dad to be happy. But what about me? I was sure she would have handled it all better than he had; at least she would have given me a little warning.

I turned back to the painting. It was too early to think about the mess my life was becoming.

Mouse and I didn't get busted until the next day.

When I opened the front door to chase down the bus that

14

morning, Julia was waiting in the driveway in her white car.

"What's she doing here?" I asked as my dad rummaged through his pockets for his keys. He looked over his shoulder and smiled at Julia.

"Ella and I thought it would be nice if you two got to know each other. So Julia's going to give you a lift to school."

"Oh." Why did parents always forget to pass on vital information?

"Have a good day at school."

"Bye, Dad." I slid into the passenger seat. "Um, thanks. Dad didn't tell me you'd be here." It's not that I didn't want a lift. I hated the bus—it always smelled like corn chips. But I just didn't know what to say to Julia. There was so much pressure: were we supposed to be best friends? Evil stepsisters? What?

"It's no problem." She shrugged. "It's on the way for me anyhow."

I looked out the window.

"It's kind of weird, isn't it?"

I nodded. "Yeah, kind of. It must suck to have to pack."

She rolled her eyes. "You have no idea. My mom's really organized. It's kind of scary sometimes."

I smiled. It felt a little awkward, but I liked the music Julia was playing. It was some retro mix.

"Cool car," I said. I was hoping for my own car this year.

"Thanks."

When we got to school, Julia's boyfriend, David, was waiting for her in the parking lot. He was tall and looked like he climbed mountains on the weekends. He was perfect for Julia. Even his teeth were perfect.

I went straight to art class. Mouse was wearing her usual odd combination of clothing: a forties-style dress she'd made herself and clunky shoes. Her bangs were short and slightly curled under to match her outfit, and she was wearing too-red lipstick. I was in my customary cargo pants and zippered sweatshirt, the same as yesterday.

I sat down behind Seth Riley. He was tall and popular and just a little sullen. I was really glad he chose art as an elective this year. Even if he no more thought of me than he thought of Ms. Harding, our art teacher. He probably thought of Harding more than me actually, since she at least gave him homework. I stared at the back of his neck, imagining his muscles beneath his sweatshirt. Pathetic, right? Mouse would never forgive me for having a crush on him. If this was even a crush. It was probably just a passing thing, like the flu. I'd just keep it to myself and hope it didn't get worse.

Ms. Harding's voice interrupted my thoughts.

"Mosaics are a very old art form, especially popular in ancient Rome. They're very easy to do. It's just a matter of gluing pieces of tile or broken glass or pottery into specific designs and then laying grout over the whole thing. Old plates are especially useful, but almost anything works: pebbles, shells, marbles, even shards of a broken mirror."

I thought of the cracked paperweight as she handed around a few books with photos of mosaic artwork. Around the room there were some examples from previous art classes. I flipped through one of the books. The mosaics were simple and pretty; all those colours, all those bits of chaos creating something cohesive and beautiful. There were Roman men in togas, mermaids, birds, spiralling waves. There were bowls, frames, tables, tiles, coasters, even frying pans covered in bits of tiles and hung on a wall.

Something tingled in my stomach. I ran my fingers over the glossy pictures. There were instructions on how to break plates by putting them in plastic bags and smashing them against the sidewalk. It sounded therapeutic.

And not nearly as weird as the way I'd been doing it.

I barely noticed when Ms. Matthews, the school secretary, poked her head in the classroom. Her gaze fell directly on Mouse.

"Victoria," she said with a sigh, "the principal would like to see you."

There were whispers, and someone hooted. Mouse stood up and took a bow. Ms. Matthews turned to me. "And you as well, Miss Perrault."

I looked down and noticed a streak of red paint on the

cuff of my sweatshirt. I took it off and stuffed it quickly into my bag. No sense being caught red-handed. I stood up and hurried to catch up to Mouse.

As I passed by Seth, I could have sworn he looked at me and smiled.

Dad came home just as I was about to dial the pizza place. It was our Friday night ritual, because neither of us wanted to cook. He always got double pepperoni and I got extra pineapple, thin crust. My stomach growled.

"Ash, I'm home," he called out.

"Hi, Dad, good timing. I was just about to order," I said. I hopped up and sat on the counter just as he came in, smiling. My cat, Grimm, jumped up too and sat on my lap.

"No pizza tonight, budgie. Ella and the girls are coming over."

I blinked. "So I'll just order an extra-large pizza."

"Ella's going to cook."

I didn't know what to say. Maybe it was stupid to be upset. It was only pizza, after all, but it was our thing. We'd been doing it since the casseroles ran out after Mom's funeral. It was important to me, but it didn't seem to be a big deal to Dad. And now it felt lame that it mattered to me so much. My hand fell away from the phone.

"They'll be here soon, but before they get here," he said,

loosening his tie, "we need to talk."

Okay, so maybe it mattered to him a little too.

"I got a phone call from your principal today, young lady."

Or not. "Oh."

"*Vandalism*, Ash?" He shook his head.

"It wasn't vandalism," I protested. Grimm was half-asleep over my knees and purring like he had a throat full of honeybees. "That mural only had men in it. Mouse and I just added some women. Like Hatshepsut and Marie Curie. If it was an art project, you would have been proud of me."

"Art projects don't generally require you to sneak into school at dawn. This could have ended very differently. You could have been suspended or even expelled. They could have made an example out of you."

"They did make an example out of me," I grumbled. "I have to help out with the dance committee and make decorations for the Halloween dance. Do you have any idea how lame that is?"

"Believe me when I say it could have been much worse."

I just stared at him. Did parents and principals get their cues from the same manual? Mr. Batra said those exact same words to us before banishing me to tissue paper and tulle and banishing Mouse to the basement to paint Pilgrims for the drama department's production of *The Crucible*.

"It was a foolish thing to do."

19

I wrinkled my nose. "It was just a stupid mural."

"Your household duties have just been increased," Dad continued. "You will vacuum. You will do laundry. You will clean the bathrooms. And you will like it."

Since those were basically the chores I had to do anyway, it didn't seem so bad. "Okay, Dad. Sorry."

"You know better than to pull a stunt like that," he said, walking out of the room. Grimm jumped off my lap and followed him.

Suddenly I wasn't all that hungry anymore.

I spent most of Saturday in my bedroom. Ella was measuring and moving things around again. It was starting to bug me, the way every single thing in the house needed adjusting. Our house didn't need re-arranging; it had worked fine for us for years.

I waited until they'd all left to go shopping before tackling my chores. I washed the kitchen floor and scrubbed the pans from breakfast. I put away my wrinkled sweaters and hung pants up in the closet. I even cleaned the mirrors in the bathroom and tried not to picture them shattering. I'd never be able to explain that.

When the kitchen was clean and the den was tidy, I went into the guest room. I forgot about the vacuuming because

I just wanted to get everything put away before Julia and Katie claimed their space. The dresser was still covered in knick-knacks on lace doilies. I taped together a cardboard box from the stack propped up against the wall and dumped everything in there.

It had been just Dad and me for five years. It would be really crowded with all those extra people coming to live with us. And what if Ella got rid of my mom's old record collection? And what if Dad let her? Okay, so we didn't even have a record player. That wasn't the point.

Not that I thought he needed my permission, but Dad might have at least mentioned he was going to marry Ella. In the movies, single parents always check in with their kids before doing this kind of thing. And in the movies, they always move in after they get married, not before.

I took the paintings down from the wall and packed them. Then I emptied the dresser of all the extra linens and packed them too. There wasn't much in the closet: a few boxes and a stack of Mom's albums. In the bottom dresser drawer I found a bundle wrapped in an old silk shawl that had belonged to my grandmother. It was heavy when I lifted it out, and I unwrapped it gingerly.

Inside were three glass birds. I hadn't seen them in years. Mom made them when I was really little when she first started taking classes in glass-blowing. I took them to my room and lined them up on the windowsill. They were plump and round as little apples, with these funny turned-in feet.

I tried not to worry about whether or not they'd be safe in my room.

Hansel and Gretel had to go through the dark woods where the old witch was waiting to eat them.

Little Red Riding Hood had to brave the moss-draped forest and the wolf to bring her grandmother cookies.

And Snow White was sitting prettily in a cottage in a wooded grove when she ate the apple.

Maybe we don't have the dark woods anymore, but we have high school, filled with wolves and witches, princesses and popular girls and boys. We have stepmothers who are perfectly nice and sometimes that just makes it worse. We have little stepsisters who are bratty.

But I think, sometimes, that the dark woods would be easier.

CHAPTER 2

It was really late, and I still couldn't sleep. I kept thinking about what I might break next. So I abandoned my cosy room and padded along the long silent hallway in my flannel pyjamas and wandered into the kitchen. I poured myself a glass of water to give me something to do, even though I wasn't really thirsty. The blue recycling box sat by the porch door, filled with empty tins and plastic containers, bits of broken cup and the cracked paperweight.

It gave me an idea.

Maybe I couldn't control what was happening when glass sort of flew apart in my presence, but at least I could do something with all the broken pieces. I could make something pretty, the way my mother had when she blew glass into bowls and vases. I loved the little birds on my windowsill.

An owl hooted softly in the backyard.

I dug under the kitchen sink until I found the grout from last spring when Dad redid the bathroom shower. I was quiet so I wouldn't wake him up. He'd only get on my case about drinking too much coffee. I borrowed some heavy-duty glue from the scissor drawer. I booted up the computer in the den, found a few websites on mosaics and printed up some instructions.

Then I lit some candles and looked around. The low coffee table would be easy. I could use a serving platter I had broken a while ago and hidden away in my closet. It had a simple purple pattern I liked. The lamps could be turned into Roman urns. I could even design coasters, little squares decorated with shattered stars. I was starting to get excited. I could see all of the patterns unfolding out of me like petals. I wondered if this was how Mom had felt when she got inspired to do glass work. It made me feel closer to her somehow.

I turned to the fireplace and tilted my head thoughtfully. It was a boring hole in the wall with a boring beige mantel. It was filled with the year-old ashes of last winter's fire. My fingers began to tingle.

Maybe Dad wouldn't mind. He and my teachers had been telling me for a long time now that I needed to find a creative outlet for my anger or my sadness or whatever emotion they wanted me to make pretty for them. He had sent me to a grief counsellor after my mom died because he hadn't known what to do with a daughter who woke up crying every night. It wasn't about the glass thing—I'd never told him about that. I'd only broken something a couple of times back then and I'd been sure there was some logical explanation. Besides, who wanted to have a therapist tell you you're nuts?

Dad wanted me to channel my emotions into something creative. And a mosaic would be definitely creative. And even though I hardly ever woke up crying anymore, I knew I needed to do something.

Ella might not like the mosaic. She might have ideas about changing the house, now that she was going to live in it. She might even *like* the boring beige fireplace. But Dad had always said the little den was mine to decorate. We never used the living room or the dining room, but I spent a lot of time on the old sofa in the den or curled up on the floor watching TV. So the fireplace was kind of mine, wasn't it?

Ideas swirled around in my head. I would edge out two lanterns burning on either side of the fireplace and use lavender and purple and blue glass for the mantelpiece. And I'd add yellow spirals and curves to illustrate candlelight. Or maybe branches covered in snow. And a bluebird in each corner, like the ones my mom and I used to watch in the backyard.

I didn't know how long it would take me, but I could at least start.

Pleased now that I had a goal, I used a pencil to mark out the pattern, sketching the lanterns and the curls of light and the birds. I laid out garbage bags to protect the floor, so Dad couldn't accuse me of making a mess.

I worked until my eyes grew bleary. I glued little pieces of crockery down, starting in one corner and working my way out. I'd found photos of a house done entirely out of mosaic. It made me dizzy to look at it, but it was beautiful too. My fingers cramped sometime after three o'clock. I fell asleep, half-wedged into the hearth.

I woke up late the next morning, my neck aching from sleeping in such a weird position. I didn't even have time for a shower. I pulled on clothes, grabbed a chocolate bar for breakfast and ran out of the house just as the bus was pulling away.

Typical.

Luckily, Julia was waiting in the driveway to pick me up.

"Are you okay?" Julia asked, as she backed her car out.

"I'm fine." I wasn't going to get into it. She'd never

understand. Though I did wonder if she missed her dad and what she thought of mine. Still, I didn't want to get all after-school-special about it. I took a bite of chocolate instead.

"You're so lucky you can eat like that," she said, looking envious. "I'd weigh three hundred pounds."

"It's chocolate," I said, as if that explained everything. "It's totally worth it."

"I wish. So are you excited about the dance?"

I blinked at her. "Uh, no. It's my detention."

It was her turn to blink.

"They're making you go to the dance as your detention?"

I snorted. "No. I have to help with the committee."

"Oh," she said as pulled up to school. "I'm helping too. I'll see you then."

It was hard to be annoyed with someone who was saving your butt. And it's not that I actually minded talking to Julia—she was nice and everything. It was just that I knew I was going to be compared to her. How was I supposed to hang around in my ratty old pyjamas eating peanut butter from the jar when she was going to be writing essays or doing the dishes or whatever? I was at a serious disadvantage.

And it was not going to escape anyone's notice.

And the way Ella and Julia got along so well kind of made me miss my mom in a way I hadn't for a long time. It's not that I didn't think of her anymore or anything, but I was ten when she died. It wasn't the same kind of missing. Sometimes I could barely remember the sound of her voice or what she smelled like. And that made me sadder than anything.

Especially since I just knew she wouldn't have expected me to be perfect like Julia. Not the woman who forgot to brush her hair on a regular basis and was always covered in grime from her studio.

School went by in a blur. When the last bell rang, the hallways became crowded with students. Laughter and voices filled the air like bats overhead. I hesitated in the entrance of the cafeteria where the first dance committee meeting was being held. The longer I stalled, the less time I'd have to spend talking streamers.

I don't think Mr. Batra realized how bad his punishment was. He'd thrown me to the wolves. A clique of beautiful, lipstick-wearing, hair-sprayed trendy wolves. I squared my shoulders. I was no meek Little Red Riding Hood. I was perfectly able to take on the wolves. And when I bit, I bit hard.

I didn't walk into the cafeteria, I marched.

I could see right away that one of the tables was filled with girls who were there just to socialize and show off, and the people who did the actual work were seated at the other table.

Outside, a bird grew disoriented and smashed into the window.

Laura glanced up from her clipboard. Beautiful Laura, with her long black hair and blue eyes. Laura, recent ex-girlfriend of Seth—beautiful boy with dark eyes and half the female population drooling at his feet. Beside her were Sophie and then Julia, looking as if she'd stepped right from the pages of a fashion magazine. Of course.

"Hey, Ash." Julia smiled at me.

Laura grimaced.

"Can we help you?" she asked, clearly doubtful.

I snorted. I was just as doubtful. "This is my detention," I said. "I'm just here to do time."

One of Laura's other friends, Michelle, raised a perfectly arched eyebrow. She wasn't gorgeous, but she was impeccably groomed. She must have had a lot of free time.

"Well, why don't you just sit down over there with the other losers and delinquents until we can find something for you to do." Laura gestured toward the other table.

I dropped onto the edge of the bench next to William.

"Hi." I stuck out my hand as if we were meeting for the first time. "Delinquent."

"Loser. Nice to meet you." He was smiling but there was a twinge of sadness to it.

"If we can get back to business?" Laura said archly, glaring in our direction. "It's important that we choose a theme today so we can get started. The dance is really soon. And this year," she paused for dramatic effect, "we get to crown a Harvest King and Queen."

Someone actually clapped in excitement. It took all kinds.

"Hey," Seth interrupted, ambling across the room and sliding onto the bench beside his friends. "Sorry I'm late."

When he caught my eye and smiled, I just blinked at him for a moment, certain it was a mistake. I hoped my smile didn't look like the grimace of a stunned deer caught in headlights.

"That's okay, Seth." Laura batted her eyelashes. I had the urge to ask her if she had a facial tic. "We all know it's a costume dance, as always. But we need a theme. Last year, Mr. Batra made us do something futuristic, and it was totally lame. This year, we're choosing for ourselves."

"How about a luau?" David suggested, winking at Julia.

"Girls in bikinis!" Noah laughed, giving him a high-five.

I rolled my eyes. This was getting off to a bad start. They didn't even know they were acting like jock stereotypes.

Sophie threw a wad of crumpled paper at them. "As if," she said. "Get a life. How about something like a masquerade, something like the eighteenth century?"

Laura tossed her hair over her shoulder. "Way too much research," she said. "We don't have enough time."

"We could do a fairy-tale theme," William suggested quietly.

"Cool," I said. A few others at our table nodded in agreement.

Laura drummed her pen on the table, ignoring us.

"Wild West?" Seth suggested.

"Bo-ring," Laura replied.

"How about William's idea?" I called out. Laura didn't even look in my direction. Seth watched me with his dark eyes. I tried not to notice, which was impossible. I spoke louder. I didn't really care what idea we went with, but I wasn't about to be ignored. "Hello? We like William's idea."

"Did we ask for your opinion?" said Laura.

"Laura." Julia sighed, then smiled at William. "Sorry, what did you say?"

Suddenly the centre of attention, William flushed. "Fairy tales," he stammered. "Y-you know, Snow White, Beauty and the Beast. That kind of thing."

"Yeah," Sophie said. "We could make it like a fairy-tale ball. Paint some towers and stuff. I think it'll be fun."

Laura looked around. "Really?"

Julia nodded. "I think it's a great idea. Hands up, those who vote yes."

Everyone's hand went up, even Laura's. Julia counted the raised hands. "Fairy tales it is."

We stayed for another half-hour until the bell rang,

discussing colours and design schemes. Laura wanted a palace, Sophie a medieval castle. No one else cared that much. They decided on a combination of both, with the ball happening in an outdoor courtyard. It would be easy to get dry ice and apples and pumpkins and throw some leaves on the ground. After that decision, Laura and Michelle began to discuss who would be Beauty and who would be Sleeping Beauty. I wanted to suggest the horse, Black Beauty.

Seth leaned over from his table and nudged me. I looked at him, one eyebrow raised, and acted like I couldn't care less.

"Way to go," he said and smiled.

I couldn't help blushing. He kept looking at me and seemed to like what he saw.

Laura glanced over, caught Seth looking at me in a way she must not have liked. "Is that ash in your hair?" she asked me. "Or mud?"

I lifted a hand to my hair before I could stop myself. *Great, must be ash from the fireplace*, I thought. I felt ridiculous. Seth hadn't been into me, he'd probably been wondering why I looked as if I'd rolled in mud.

"I guess it's obvious who you'll be dressing up as," Laura continued. "But it's not much of a stretch, is it, Cinderella?"

The bottle of cranberry juice in front of Laura cracked suddenly and splattered all over her white shirt. She shrieked and leaped to her feet. Everyone jumped up and moved away from the table.

I snuck away so no one would see me smirking.

I probably should have felt bad.

But I so didn't.

There was potential here. Lots and lots of potential.

I heard footsteps behind me on the stairs.

"Ash," Seth said. "Wait up."

I stopped and turned, waiting under the image of Anne Boleyn. There was a line of red at her throat. Mouse definitely had a gruesome sense of humour sometimes. I shifted from foot to foot.

"Yeah?" I asked.

Seth nodded his head to the mural. "I heard you and Mouse painted it. That true?"

I nodded. "Yeah. Decorating committee is my detention."

He winced. "Rough."

"Aren't they your friends?"

"Some of them. Sometimes." He closed the distance between us.

My mouth felt dry. "Did you want something?" I finally asked. I couldn't help thinking of the ash in my hair.

"Just to say hi," he said. He pushed a strand of Kool-Aid coloured hair off my forehead. "Hi."

My heart felt like a bird beating its wings.

I heard the screech of soles on linoleum as someone stopped abruptly, rounding the corner. Mouse squeaked. "Ash."

I wondered if strangling my best friend would be a crime in this situation.

"I'll see you after school, I guess," Seth said, stepping back.

I could only nod.

"Seth, man, where are you?" David shouted from the cafeteria.

"Bye." Seth winked.

Mouse waited until he was out of earshot. "Ash Cynthia Perrault, have you lost your mind?"

They say he's handsome and polished and has a really shiny suit of armour. They say all the girls want to marry him, or at least dance with him and wear his red-rose corsage pinned to their dress.

They say he searched and searched the land for her, riding from village to village, sleeping in the mud, crossing narrow bridges, fighting trolls.

Well, he sent his best men anyway.

I wonder if he would have tried as hard if her hands had smelled like the onions she'd chopped for dinner or she had mud on her dress. If she wasn't particularly pretty, just clever and wild.

And if she never wore dresses, just old cargo pants.

CHAPTER 3

"Seth Riley?" Mouse repeated for the hundredth time as we walked down the street toward the art supply shop. When I'd demonstrated enthusiasm for mosaics, Ms. Harding had piled me with bags of old tiles and given me a list of what supplies I'd need and where to get them. I already knew the art shop. It was on the same block as Mocha Palace, where Mouse, Nicholas and I hung out.

Mouse shook her head, still on the subject of Seth. "He's so...ordinary."

"Just because he's not into guerrilla warfare doesn't make him ordinary," I said. I wanted to enjoy the fact that Seth knew I was alive, not debate his relative merits with Mouse.

"It does so," Mouse replied around a mouthful of red liquorice. Today she was dressed vaguely like a Gibson girl, in a narrow skirt and a lace blouse. There was a cameo on a black ribbon around her neck. "I just don't get it."

"Nothing happened," I insisted as we went into the store. The bells on the door jingled softly.

"Something might have."

"But it didn't." But was it wrong that I kind of wished something *had* happened?

Mouse shook her head. "Ash, you know what Seth's like. Do you really find him attractive? Plus, he's on the rebound. *Again.*"

I rolled my eyes. "I know. It's weird. But he's cute. I can't help it." I wasn't an idiot. I knew Seth wasn't a saint. But he wasn't anything other than nice to me.

"You're not going to get all emo over him are you?"

Mouse was so melodramatic sometimes. I rolled my eyes again. "It's no big deal. Now help me look for the mosaic stuff, okay?"

I grabbed a basket and we wandered up and down aisles filled with pencils and paintbrushes and stacks of white canvases. There was a whole corner devoted to mosaic supplies: tiles, tile cutters, grout, adhesive and books. There were little bags filled with smalti and polished pebbles and vitreous glass, which was the cheapest glass and therefore the kind I decided to buy. I filled my basket and hovered indecisively over the books. I could only afford one. I was dipping into the very last of my summer babysitting money as it was, and I had vowed never to babysit again. Maybe I would ask for a gift certificate to the art store for my birthday.

When I was done and we were back outside, Mouse pulled out another roll of liquorice.

"I still want to know who squealed on us," she muttered.

"Like it wasn't obvious from the start," I replied.

She made a face. "I guess."

Born Victoria Piercy, Mouse had earned her nickname last year, in her very first week at school, when she freed all of the mice from the science lab. She was still serving detention for that little escapade. By the time the mice had made warm snuggly homes for themselves in the walls, Mouse had nearly been suspended. Nobody had to squeal on Mouse. Whenever a prank happened at Newcastle High, everyone knew that she was involved.

When we got to Mouse's house, we kicked off our boots in the front hall, and after fixing a snack, we climbed the stairs to her room. Her parents weren't home yet, and there was no one to disapprove of our choice of hot fudge sundaes as pre-dinner appetizers.

Mouse's room was literally buried under bolts of fabrics and reams of thread. Every corner was a multi-coloured web.

Her desk saw more sewing than homework. She tended to study sprawled on her bed so she wouldn't disturb her sewing machine, which she'd named Ariadne.

She turned on her stereo and played a Kate Bush album. Mouse was in a retro mood again.

"Have you started studying for your learner's permit yet?"

I thought about the wide expanse of windshield glass and could see it cracking.

"Um, no." I leaned back against the pillows and changed the subject. "How was painting scenery for the play?"

She scooped up a spoonful of ice cream. "Dull, though at least the drama geeks are interesting. And I got some totally cool tips on costume design books. Need I ask about the dance decorations?"

"Mean girls," I said. "Nothing unusual there. We're going with a fairy-tale theme."

She nodded slowly. "That doesn't completely suck."

"What's your costume?"

"I'm sure I don't know."

"You so didn't wait until we chose a theme, Mouse. You were up to your eyeballs in velvet the first day you heard it was a costume dance."

Mouse put on an innocent face. "Who, me?"

I smirked. "Anne Boleyn or Robin Hood?"

She pouted, crossing her arms. "You peeked."

I laughed. "Are you kidding? I've known you forever,

Piercy. It couldn't be anything else."

"Maybe I'm going as Marie Antoinette."

"Please. You'd never dress up as someone who didn't fight for the poor and the hungry, even if she was a queen and had her head lopped off."

Mouse nodded thoughtfully. "I do have a thing about beheaded queens. Think I should see a doctor?"

"Definitely."

We grinned at each other.

"So?" I asked after we'd licked the last of the hot fudge out of our bowls. "Did you get in trouble with your mom for the mural thing?"

"From the woman who went into labour with me while in jail for protesting old-growth logging? Are you kidding?"

"I wish my dad had that kind of attitude," I said.

"Are you still my date for the dance? Or are you grounded?" Mouse asked.

I thought of Seth. He would probably never ask me to the dance. I could ask him, but why set myself up for humiliation? Never mind that Laura would probably claw my eyes out.

"I don't think anyone else is going to ask me," I said finally.

I spent most of my spares in the art room finishing a small

mosaic plate with a ring of glass marbles in the centre where you could rest a cup or a glass. The marbles were from the vase filled with coloured glass my mom had kept in the guest bathroom. I thought Dad could use the plate as a coaster in his office. I made a mess with the grout, but I did get the hang of it eventually.

I gave the plate to him after school while we were waiting to go out for dinner for Katie's birthday. I'd put it in a box and then tied the box up with a blue ribbon. It was my first finished mosaic. I was really proud of it.

"Dad, I made something for you."

He looked up distractedly from where he was standing at the front hall mirror, fiddling with his tie. "What's that, budgie? Oh, remember to be extra nice to Katie tonight. She's younger than you, and this might all be confusing for her."

Please. Katie knew exactly what was going on and was far less confused about it than me.

"Here." I handed him the box, not wanting to discuss the ready-made family about to move in. "I made it."

"A present for me? Are you buttering me up for something?" he teased.

I grinned. "No."

"Well, thanks, I'll…" He was reaching for the blue ribbon when the front door opened. There wasn't a knock and the doorbell didn't ring. Ella and her daughters walked in.

Dad's hand reached out to touch Ella. She smiled and kissed him warmly. The rest of us looked away. The hallway was suddenly cramped.

"Happy birthday!" Dad said and lifted Katie up into a bear hug until she squealed. "My girls all look so beautiful tonight. I'm such a lucky guy."

Katie grinned. She looked at my wrinkled T-shirt. "Are you wearing that?" she asked.

"Yeah. So?" I looked down at myself. I'd put on a long skirt—this was as fancy as I got. Next thing, they'd expect me to wear those rickety heels. I didn't think so. Julia, of course, was wearing a knee-length skirt that flared out at the hem and a smart little jacket. Perfect for her, but for me, a perfect nightmare.

"Maybe you should dress up a little," Dad said to me. "It is a special occasion, after all." This from the man who would wear his bathrobe to work if they let him.

I frowned. Hadn't I been one of his lovely girls just a minute ago?

"There's no time," Ella said, tapping her watch. "We're going to be late if we don't leave now."

We piled into Dad's car, which suddenly filled with three different types of perfume. It made me vaguely nauseous. I rolled my window down. Dad's present sat on my lap. He had forgotten to bring it with him.

The restaurant was one of those nice places where they

take your coat for you and unfold your napkin and put it on your lap. You know, in case you don't know what a napkin is for. Candles burned on every table. The menu was in English and Italian. Katie loved spaghetti above all else— above the latest boy band, the latest movie celebrity and the latest iPod cover.

For my birthday, all I wanted was pizza. And root-beer floats and a stack of bad zombie movies.

Everyone talked all through dinner. Apparently, there was going to be an engagement party soon. No one mentioned my birthday, which was coming up. I ate my pesto and garlic bread and didn't say very much, but no one seemed to notice. Julia ate a green salad. I ate enough carbs and fat for both of us. When the plates were cleared and the chocolate mousse cake was finished, the presents came out. Julia left most of her cake on her plate, playing with her fork the entire time. What a sad waste of chocolate. The least she could have done was pass her dessert over to me. It was then that I realized I didn't actually have a present for Katie. Was I supposed to? Nobody had told me, and we'd never done presents before as a group. Katie ripped through her presents: a silver bracelet from her mom, a purple sweater from Julia and a new cellphone from my dad. I blinked when everyone looked at me.

"Uh…"

"Oh, here's your present from Ash," my dad broke in.

And he handed Katie the box I'd slipped to him when we sat down.

"But..."

He nudged me pointedly. I didn't know why, but I suddenly felt like crying.

"Ash made it herself."

But I'd made it for him. I didn't know what to do, so I just sat there.

Katie tore off the ribbon and opened the box. "It's a plate," she said.

"Did you mosaic that yourself?" Ella asked quickly. I nodded. "It's beautiful," she added.

Dad just smiled. The waiter came and handed him the bill, and then it was time to go home. As I pulled my jacket on, Dad's wineglass wobbled and tipped over. The stain spread all over the tablecloth. Dad paused, looked at me. I swallowed, looking back at him. I hadn't touched the glass, but I didn't know if he'd believe me. His expression was wary, as if he wasn't sure whether he should be mad or not.

Katie rolled her eyes. "You're so clumsy."

I emailed Mouse as soon as I got home.

    This sucks. I deserve chocolate.

I waited impatiently for her to reply. I scrolled up and down the page once before emailing again.

> Mouse, stop looking at mouldy old dress patterns and answer me already!

She emailed me back almost right away.

> *How did you know?*

> Please, that's all you do online.

> *Let's go to the Palace Saturday night. I'll buy you one of those chocolate gingerbread men and you can bite its head off.*

> I am so there.

Saturday afternoon the house was blessedly empty. I decided to take advantage of it while I still could. I went into the den and glued chips of blue and purple glass along the pattern pencilled on the mantelpiece. It was calming, the way I imagined meditation was supposed to be if I could ever sit still long enough, and there was no way Dad could ignore the fireplace like he had the coaster. I loved everything about mosaics: snipping the tiles, gluing them into a precise pattern, like a puzzle. Everything fit in its place, everything had a purpose.

After about an hour, I had to stop. I'd run out of blue, and I wanted bluebirds at each corner. I checked the recycling box but there was nothing in there but pop cans. I even searched under the sink but only found the phone book, a watering can and cleaning products. I noticed the coffeemaker was on the other counter instead of by the sink. The new kitchen table was a little too big, but the wood was smooth and unstained. There were five chairs around it. Weird.

My eyes fell on the shelf over the microwave. It held a wilting ivy plant, dusty candles and one of those tacky photo-transfer plates. My mom had it made at a carnival. It showed a photo of me when I was eight, two years before the drunk driver hit her car. My hair was long and blond and dandelion-yellow. I was wearing a blue sweater. I had a goofy smile and was eating a huge vanilla ice cream cone.

Next to it was a red bowl, with delicate edges like a lily.

Or that's what should have been next to it.

Instead, the space was empty, clear of dust and any lingering traces of my mother—of the fact that she'd been a glass artist or that her favourite colour was red. "Unbelievable," I muttered. It was one thing to move the couch; it was another thing entirely to remove my mother's bowl without asking me.

The crows in the garden were cawing, screaming. I glanced out the window. They lifted into the air like a storm cloud. The glasses in the cupboard shook. I looked back at the shelf.

I grabbed the plate with the photo of me on it and went into the den. The sweater, once broken, would become blue feathers. For some reason, all that mattered was that I finish the damned fireplace. And I couldn't stand that little girl, all innocent and cute. Glass didn't break around her.

I heaved the plate into the fireplace.

In the old stories, magic seems so simple.

It's just another part of the pattern, like rain or birthday presents. Simple. A spell for sleep, feathers that transform you into a bird, red shoes that won't stop dancing.

And there are always warnings.

If you're paying attention.

CHAPTER 4

The Mocha Palace was a favourite hangout for the alternative crowd from the surrounding high schools. Most of the crowd was pierced, tattooed or wearing Goth granny boots. The walls were Moroccan blue and the ceiling glimmered with silver stars. The tables were old wood with candles burning in red glass jars. A torn velvet couch sat against one wall. A painting hung above it in an ornate gilded frame. The Palace always smelled like incense and ground coffee beans.

Mouse, Nicholas and William were in one of the booths tucked by the back window. I slid in beside Mouse.

"I hate my life," I said.

Mouse snorted. "You don't hate your life until you've painted Pilgrims with dorky hats for three hours every day for some stupid school play."

Nicholas raised an eyebrow. "Challenge extended," he said.

They looked at me, waiting for my reason. It almost made me smile.

"I did chores all day. And we have new furniture and everything's in the wrong place." I didn't mention the rest.

Nicholas made a so-so gesture with his hand.

"I've heard better, Perrault."

I didn't say anything.

"Ash, seriously, are you okay?" Mouse touched the back of my fingers.

"I'm fine." I jerked away and slid out of the booth. I didn't want to sound crazy. "I'm getting a drink. Want anything?"

When they shook their heads, I left for the counter. I knew they were talking about me. It was easy for them. Mouse had more confidence than ten cats and nothing ever bothered Nicholas. They just didn't get it. No one did.

I cradled my chai latte gently as a baby bird, afraid the mug might shatter in my hands. When I returned to the booth I wanted to apologize for snapping at Mouse, but I was still too tense, too tight. My teeth felt like I'd been clenching them for weeks. I offered Mouse my chocolate cupcake as a peace offering. As a return peace offering, she let me eat half.

"So Mr. Batra and the whole faculty have gone insane," I said, once we'd licked all the icing off our forks. I just wanted it to be a normal night, a fun night.

Mouse blinked. "Weren't they always?"

"Not like this. Apparently, they think we all need more school spirit. They've decided to start a new tradition: crowning a Harvest King and Queen."

"What?" Mouse squeaked in outrage. Nicholas and I exchanged a glance and sat back in our seats. There was nothing like a good Mouse rant. William was in for a treat. "That's antiquated and ridiculous. That doesn't foster school spirit, just competition and unhealthy, fascist beauty standards. It's the beginning of the year, it's too early for this shit. Do you think for one second the Harvest King or Queen are going to have pimples? Or a fat butt? I want a Queen with a fat butt."

I laughed so hard chai tea came out of my nose.

And then Seth Riley walked in, just in time to hear me snort.

Of course.

When he smiled at me, I kind of stared at him like he had three heads. I'd never seen him here before. It didn't seem like his type of place. I'd heard he spent most of his time in the back seat of his car with some pretty girl. But instead he was sitting in a funky coffeehouse in his jeans and shaggy hair and smiling at me.

"Um," I chugged the last of my tea. "I'm…gonna get another one."

I made sure I walked by Seth on my way to the counter. I slowed down, but I wouldn't stop unless he talked to me. I wasn't going to embarrass myself.

"Ash." He stood up, smiling.

I swallowed. "Oh. Hey, Seth." There. That was nice and casual. It would be easier if I didn't know Mouse was watching us so suspiciously.

"Is he your boyfriend?" He nodded toward Nicholas.

I blinked. So much for casual. "No."

"That William guy?"

"No."

His smile widened. I wondered if this was a joke and there was some secret camera filming my reactions. Before I could ask that very question, I blurted out the second thing that came to mind. "I didn't think you usually hung out here."

"I don't. I came to see you."

"Oh."

"Is that okay?"

Are you kidding? I wanted to ask. *Have you seen yourself lately?* Instead I just half-smiled and shrugged. "Sure."

"Can I walk you home?"

"Sure."

I turned my back and widened my eyes at Mouse, equally panicked and excited. I waved goodbye. She narrowed her eyes but waved back. I could only imagine what she was thinking as she watched her best friend leave with one of the most popular and dangerous guys at school. The kind of guy that went for glamour girls in miniskirts, not girls in ripped cargos. I was sure she'd come to our usual conclusion: guys just didn't make sense.

"Girls just don't make sense," Nicholas muttered as I followed Seth outside.

We didn't speak at first, just walked along the sidewalk. I was worried that the silence would stretch on awkwardly and irrevocably.

The night smelled of rain and trees. In the streetlight, the leaves skittered across the road like spiders. Seth reached for my hand. His skin was warm. I nearly stopped walking altogether.

Play it cool, I told myself sternly. *It's no big deal.*

No big deal? I argued back. *Seth Riley is touching me. Are you not paying attention?*

Seth glanced at me, smiling, and led me into an empty park. The swings gleamed, creaking in the wind. The river meandered nearby, crackling like tin foil. I saw a crane, grey and still as a ghost. Seth stopped and turned to me.

He tilted his head, brushing his fingers over my cheek, leaning in to kiss me. Suddenly, voices cut through the park and he paused, his mouth hovering an inch from mine. My eyes flew open. Seth frowned. I recognized the voices too—some of his friends from school, laughing and being loud as they passed by on the sidewalk.

"Woo-hoo," one of them whistled, seeing our shadows so close together. Seth tensed, but they kept whistling and hollering. He was starting to ease away, and I had to stop myself from grabbing him. Frustration hummed through me. I glared at the streetlight near us. It cast too much light, would give us away and ruin the moment completely. I glared harder until the streetlight cracked with a loud pop.

This glass thing might be scary, but sometimes it was kind of cool too.

Shadow enveloped us, and I felt Seth relax. He glanced up, clearly assuming that the bulb had burned out with excellent timing. When his friends walked away, bored now that we were mostly hidden, he relaxed further. They hadn't recognized us. He kissed me then, grinning. His mouth was clever, practised. It made the blood rush down into my thighs. Our breaths mingled, tongues touching gently. The last streetlight popped.

I didn't see Seth at school on Monday, which was probably

a good thing. I was still giddy about the kiss. I'd always assumed he barely knew I even existed. The last time he'd actually spoken to me was back in grade three. He had pulled my hair and told me I was ugly.

Had he actually kissed me in the dark when the sky was thick with stars? I was half-afraid to think about it, to talk about it, as if I might jinx it.

Damn. I was getting all dopey over a guy. It was kind of nice though. When I was thinking about Seth, I wasn't thinking about stepmothers and weddings and glass shattering. Ordinarily I would have prattled on to Mouse about the way Seth's hair fell over his forehead. That's what best friends were for, they listened to you make an ass out of yourself. But Mouse didn't like Seth, and I didn't want to let go of the glow.

And, okay, I might have reacted the same way if Mouse had suddenly started dating Jackson or Noah. But those guys tripped people in the hallway. Seth wasn't like that.

I wasn't sure what that kiss meant. I didn't intend to get all stupid and follow after him asking if I was his girlfriend now. But I wanted to know.

Granted, I didn't have a boatload of kisses to compare Seth's kiss to, but enough to know that this was different. It was nothing like that wet sloppy mess Derek had planted on me behind the gym last year. Seth clearly had lots of practice. I had none, Derek notwithstanding.

Dating just wasn't my thing. It all seemed like too much work, worrying about what your hair looked like and if a certain boy noticed and whether or not he would call you that night. But now I kind of wished I'd had more practice dating guys. Seth wasn't exactly my boyfriend, but we were dating, weren't we?

I realized after a long moment of sitting there with a goofy grin that I was staring at a cup full of chocolate dregs. It was one of the glass mugs, the ones you buy at department stores. I held it in my hand, considering. The glass thing wasn't getting any less freaky. Maybe it was just some sort of odd coincidence. I sighed. There was no way it was a coincidence. Glass didn't just break itself sitting there on the shelf. Which meant what exactly? I might have asked Dad about it, but I wasn't stupid. He wasn't going to believe me, not about something as weird as this. It was probably best all around if I kept my mouth shut.

I put the cup down at a safe distance and then stared at it, willing it to crack, the way the streetlight had cracked. I willed it to shatter into pieces. I willed it to break and fall apart.

I willed it to do *anything* until I was red in the face and panting. Nothing.

Nothing at all.

My eyes hurt, and I felt like an idiot. The cup was still a cup. I didn't have special powers. I couldn't do cool things like break juice bottles or streetlamps.

A small round chickadee with black and white markings landed on my windowsill. His eyes were like tiny seeds. I leaned forward slowly so I wouldn't startle him. He tilted his head and made an inquisitive sort of sound. I sat there for a long time.

He just stayed where he was too, watching me and pecking at the glass.

Another dance committee meeting. As expected, Laura was walking around with her clipboard and white blouse like she was in charge of everything, which she wasn't. I ignored her and went over to help William cut stars out of blue construction paper. They would be brushed with glitter and punched with a hole so they could hang from the ceiling on the night of the dance. The other students were measuring out squares to paint grey so they would look like stones. Seth was laughing with Noah over paint. When Noah stood up to get more water for the brushes, I wandered over and crouched down next to Seth.

"Hey."

He glanced at me.

"Hey." He didn't say anything else, just moved his brush over a square that was already thick with wet paint. I wasn't sure what to do. He wouldn't look at me, and I was afraid I'd imagined the kiss. Maybe I was supposed to act casual and cool. But I needed some kind of contact. I pushed my hair back and leaned into him so that our arms were close.

"Is everything okay?" I asked him quietly.

He shifted away slightly. "Sure."

I stood up. I knew when I was being ignored.

"You're acting weird."

He shrugged. "I'm just busy." He smiled with relief when Noah returned. "Hey, man. Have you asked Leah out yet?"

It was a clear dismissal. Before I could even figure out how to react, Laura walked over. She smiled so sweetly I thought I might go into insulin shock. "Are you lost, Cinderslut?"

I blinked.

"What?" I was not in the mood for this.

Laura's smile sharpened. "The freaks and geeks are over there." She pointed to the people I usually hung out with. "So run along."

Just then, Julia came to stand behind me.

"Laura," she said, with a hint of anger.

I shook my head. I didn't want her to be nice to me or to stand up for me. Seth just sat there and didn't say anything.

"Whatever." I turned my back and bit the inside of my cheek hard so my lip wouldn't tremble. I do *not* cry in public, I reminded myself. And definitely not over Laura's idea of an insult.

Angry, I stomped down the hall toward my locker. It felt good to hear the slap of my boots on the floor. I yanked open my locker, cursing as a math book popped out and hit my knee. I picked it up and slammed it back inside. I kicked the door shut again and saw Seth, waiting.

"Ash."

I walked away, my mouth tight. He followed me into the dark stairwell. I thought I saw the edge of Mouse's purple sequin skirt near the top, mostly out of view, but I couldn't be sure. I headed up toward it.

"Ash, wait."

I stopped and huffed out an impatient breath. "What?" I snapped.

"I'm sorry."

"You ignored me, Seth. And you just sat there when Laura went off."

"I know. I'm sorry. But we just broke up, you know? She's taking it hard that I dumped her."

I didn't say anything. The last thing I wanted was to be reminded of him and Laura. I thought about them in the halls last year, holding hands and laughing.

"You just caught me off guard," he continued. "My friends don't know about us."

"About us what?"

He leaned back against the wall. "It's complicated. I just don't want to rub it in Laura's face, you know?"

63

I softened slightly. Not because I cared about Laura, but because he touched my hand. He pulled me closer, tipped my chin up. The way he looked at me made me feel like I was the only thing in the world worth looking at. "Okay?"

I wasn't sure what I wanted, but it seemed easier to give in. The kiss was long and gentle, distracting.

For right now, it was perfect.

The morning Ella, Julia and Katie moved in was sunny and clear. The trees looked like they were on fire. The moving truck pulled up the driveway before eight o'clock. I was still in my pyjamas and sitting bleary-eyed over a cup of coffee. Dad was dressed and caffeinated. He even clapped his hands when he heard the truck doors slam. "They're here!" If he'd been a six-year-old boy hearing Santa Claus on the roof, he couldn't have looked happier. "Ash, hurry up and get dressed."

By the time I was presentable, there was already a parade of movers tramping up and down the hallway, toting boxes and furniture. Katie put a horrid, pink furry chair next to her desk in the guest room. Paintings came down, and new ones went up. Boxes full of clothes and books were piled everywhere. Dad's bed got moved out even though there was nothing wrong with it, and a new one was moved in.

I mostly tried to stay out of the way until I was accused of not helping. So I dutifully went into the kitchen to unpack dishes and load them into the dishwasher to be cleaned. We already had dishes. Apparently, our old mismatched plates were an affront to the decorating gods. It was totally unfair that I had to be polite. If I'd gone into someone's house and insulted the dishes, the carpet and the couch, I would have got into trouble. Adults had it easy. They made the rules and they broke them whenever they felt like it. Meanwhile, I had to figure out where to store all the extra stuff in our small kitchen. It wasn't easy.

After that, I carried so many boxes into the storage room that the muscles in my legs began to ache. I stole a few minutes in the basement to catch my breath. I wasn't used to so many people in the house.

When Dad hollered down that they'd just ordered pizza, I went back upstairs. I escaped to the den, but Katie was already in there. She was moving my CDs around. I'd spent hours putting them in alphabetical order.

"Hey!" I said.

She jumped and looked over her shoulder. She was wearing a yellow T-shirt, jeans and flip-flops a couple of sizes too big for her.

"Oh, hey," she said, deliberately misinterpreting my "hey" as a greeting.

"I already cleared a shelf for you." There were boxes piled all around us like mini-castle walls. You couldn't move without stubbing a toe.

"I know, but I need more space."

I folded my arms. "Too bad, kid. We each get a shelf."

"I'm not a kid," she flared, insulted. She kicked the bucket of tiles by the fireplace. "If you moved all this junk, we'd have more room."

I just looked at her steadily. "It's not junk. It's art," I replied. "It stays."

She huffed out a sigh. "Mom says we all have to compromise."

"I've compromised," I said through my teeth.

"I'm telling."

"Go ahead." The joys of having a younger stepsister. She flounced off in a snit. It was kind of impressive to watch.

At least, until the glass on the table broke into pieces with a pop like a pellet gun. I jumped. Katie, startled, tripped and couldn't catch her balance. She tumbled over a cardboard box and fell down with a crash. It happened so fast, I barely had time to blink. A flip-flop flew off and landed by my foot. They were my house flip-flops, the ones I used as slippers. I could tell because they had a coffee stain shaped like Italy on the sole.

Katie started to cry and shout for her mom. Ella and Dad rushed in before I'd even taken two steps.

"What happened?" Ella helped Katie up, who was crying harder.

"She fell over one of the boxes," I explained.

"She was mean to me!" Katie sniffled. "She wouldn't let me have a shelf."

"Ash, I asked you to clear space for the girls," Dad said.

"Dad, I *did*. We each get one, like you said." I couldn't believe I was having to defend myself. Had he forgotten I was his flesh and blood?

"It really hurts!" Katie said, holding onto her foot.

"Can you stand on it?" Dad asked.

Katie tried to stand up and shrieked, "Ow! Mom! It's broken! Ow!"

Ella clucked her tongue and hooked her arm around Katie's shoulder. "It does look swollen, honey. Probably sprained."

"It hurts!" Katie wailed. "It's her fault. She did it!" she added, all but howling. "She threw a glass at me and it broke, and I got startled and fell."

Dad frowned at me.

My mouth dropped open. I felt bad for Katie, but I wasn't going to take the blame for her clumsiness. "What? I did not!"

But I knew by the way he was looking at me that Dad was remembering the broken shards in the recycling box and the wine glass at dinner the other night. "Ash, is this true?"

"No!"

"Ash."

"Dad! I would never throw a glass at her!" My own father didn't believe me. I must have looked guilty because Dad's face changed.

"Ash, get some ice," he barked at me. "Now."

Muttering under my breath, I ran to the kitchen and dumped out one of the ice trays. When I returned, Dad and Ella were helping Katie hobble to the front door.

"We're going to take you to the hospital, honey. Everything will be okay," Ella murmured as I followed them with a towel of ice.

"Here," I said. "Should I come too?"

Dad didn't even look at me.

"I think you've done enough for today."

Where the hell's my fairy godmother?

Because if she's coming at all, she's clearly stuck in traffic.

And it's not like I want her to count spilled lentils or send birds to sew me a pretty dress or get me a date for the dance. That stuff's easy. Well, everything but the date part.

What I want is for her to fix all the stuff that actually needs fixing. Like fathers who don't see you, not really, and boys that don't see you, not really, and not being able to see yourself, not really.

Come to think of it, she's probably not coming after all. She's probably too busy making diamond tiaras and carriages out of large vegetables. I ask you, how is that helpful?

Damn it.

That means I'm going to have to fix all this stuff myself.

CHAPTER 5

I met Mouse and Nicholas at the Palace. I ordered a large gooey chocolate cupcake and an extra-large mochaccino. I'd have to try and get home before they all got back from the hospital, otherwise Dad might take my absence as proof of my guilt. Even though he should know better. I still couldn't believe he'd looked at me like that, all accusing and disappointed, as if he didn't know who I was. I felt tears burning behind my eyes just thinking about it.

Mouse and Nicholas were sitting closer to each other than usual. I frowned.

"Hey, what's going on?"

Mouse looked up. "Oh. Hi, Ash."

Nicholas slid over. His hair was standing on end like he'd been jerking his hand through it, which he only did when he was nervous. "I was just showing Mouse the new lyrics I wrote," he said.

I nodded and sat down, precariously balancing my cup and plate. "Cool." I ate half the cupcake before I said another word.

"Bad day," Mouse said knowingly, watching me lick icing off the corner of my mouth.

"Beyond crappy."

"What happened?"

"Not only is it moving day, but Katie sprained her ankle. She's at the emergency room."

"Is she okay?" Nicholas asked.

"She's fine. They called to say it was just a mild sprain." Once I'd heard that, I'd hightailed it out of the house. "And apparently it's all my fault because she tripped over a box," I grumbled. "She says I threw stuff at her."

"What?" Mouse said. "That's just stupid."

I swear I could have kissed her right then and there. My own father didn't believe me, but at least my best friend did.

"Mouse, will you marry me?" I joked.

She batted her eyelashes. "Well, I don't know. I'm in such high demand." She hugged me. "Never mind about that other stuff," she said. "It's over now. We can wallow in sugar until our teeth fall out."

I smiled lazily. "That sounds nice."

Nicholas rubbed his teeth gingerly. "You have a weird idea of what's nice."

"I hang out with you, don't I?" I said. He kicked me lightly under the table. "Besides, you eat wheat germ and seaweed and shit. That is *not* nice."

"Hey," he protested. "This body is a temple."

Mouse and I both laughed.

"Jackson's having a party," Nicholas added before I could start in on his conviction that organic honey cured hay fever. "We should go."

"When?"

"Tonight. You in?"

I nodded. A party could be fun. And Seth might be there. Mouse squeaked.

"I have to go home and make a new outfit."

Nicholas and I both groaned. Mouse spent hours and hours creating and altering outfits.

"What?" she asked innocently.

"So we'll see you sometime after midnight then?"

She stuck out her tongue. "It won't take me that long." She perked up. "I could make something for you."

"Oh, my God, we'll never see her again," Nicholas said.

I lifted my hands in horror. "Do *not* make me an outfit."

She pouted. "I'm a good seamstress."

"You're an excellent seamstress," I agreed. "But I wear cargo pants."

"But it's a party."

"Cargo pants," I insisted.

I got home a few minutes before Dad and Ella and Katie. I threw my jacket onto my bed. Katie hobbled in with crutches. Her ankle was wrapped in a tensor-bandage. Her eyes were still red from crying. My father and Ella followed closely behind her.

I felt nervous even though I knew it wasn't my fault. Not on purpose anyway. The glass breaking was because of me, but it wasn't like I could do it on command. It just sort of happened. Not exactly something I could explain.

"Ash, I'd like to talk to you in the kitchen."

I swallowed. Ella helped Katie into the den and turned on the television for her. Julia, who'd come out to say hello, disappeared back into her room. Then Ella rejoined me and Dad in the kitchen. The shards of the broken glass she held were blue as wood violets. Dad's mouth tightened.

"I can't believe a daughter of mine would behave like this."

I slumped in my chair. "Dad, I did *not* throw a glass at her!"

"Then explain this." He pointed to the broken pieces.

Ella tossed them into the recycling box.

"Just as soon as you explain to me why you won't believe me!" I replied angrily.

"Cynthia Ash Perrault, watch your tone, young lady."

My full name and a "young lady." I was doomed.

"Katie said that you threw the glass at her. Are you saying she was lying?" Ella asked quietly.

"No," I said, even though I wanted to say yes. "Well, kind of."

Dad pinched the bridge of his nose. "Help me out here, Ash," he said with a bit more suspicion than I think I warranted. I was his daughter after all. "If you didn't break the glass, how did it happen?"

"For one thing she was already tripping, from wearing my shoes, by the way, without asking."

"Focus."

I really thought I might snarl. Didn't he hear me at all? This was so totally unfair. I swallowed back tears. "Dad. She tripped, maybe she knocked the table and the glass fell over. *I don't know.*"

Dad and Ella exchanged glances. It made me madder.

"Ash, please leave us alone. Ella and I need to talk. You're grounded."

"But there's a party tonight!"

"You're not going to any party."

I jumped to my feet. To my horror, I felt my lower lip

tremble. "Dad! Please!"

He shook his head.

I gulped back a sob and ran down the hall, slamming my door behind me. The whole wall shook. It only made me feel marginally better. This whole weekend just plain sucked. I threw myself on the bed and sulked. I must have fallen asleep, because when I woke up the sun had set. And I was still grounded. Seth would be at the party and some other girl would be there to kiss him.

Not going to happen.

I pulled a crocheted sweater over my tank top and brushed my hair. I even added some eyeliner, which I rarely wore. It was black and smudged and kind of looked like I was going for the zombie effect, but I liked it.

I had no intention of staying grounded. I waited until David picked Julia up for the party, waited until Katie went to bed, waited until Ella turned the lights out.

Then I climbed out my window. There were definite advantages to living in a bungalow. I landed half in the rose bush but managed not to swear out loud when thorns scraped across the back of my hand.

Mouse was almost ready, since I was so late. That meant Nicholas and I only had to watch one bad sitcom and the end of the news while we waited for her.

When a commercial came on, Nicholas glanced at me. "What's up, Perrault?" he asked.

"Nothing."

He made a face at me. "Those people on the news with the house fire looked happier than you do right now."

"I don't want to talk about it."

"Talk about what?" Mouse shouted down from the top of the stairs.

"Why she's so morose," Nicholas shouted back.

I didn't want their pity, but I knew them well enough to know that neither of them would let up until I gave them an answer.

"I'm grounded tonight," I finally said. "I snuck out."

"Oh, Ash. Your dad's gonna freak," Mouse said, as she started down the stairs.

I shook my head. "Not if he doesn't find out." It still really hurt that Dad hadn't listened to me. "Look, can we please not talk about it? I just want to forget the whole day ever happened."

Mouse was wearing an Edwardian style shirt in black with white lace ruffles. It was only partially buttoned over a silk slip that went to her knees, over a pair of jean capris. Her red hair was up in a messy bun with curls slipping out, dusted with glitter. She looked good.

"Nice," Nicholas said, letting out a low whistle and nudging me with his shoulder.

For a minute I thought she might be blushing, but it must have been the bad lighting. Mouse never blushed, and especially not around Nicholas, whom we'd known since I'd sat on him and made him eat mud in kindergarten.

"Thanks," Mouse said softly.

"Are we ready?" I shook my head at them. They were acting weird.

Luckily, Jackson lived just down the street, so we walked. The moon was teasing us, pouring out pale light between fitful clouds. I thought I heard an owl in one of the maple trees. Jackson's parents were away, so all the lights were blazing, and the house was packed. We could feel the thump of the music in the driveway pavement. We eased our way inside through the crowd at the front door.

I looked around for Seth, but I couldn't see him. His friends were hanging around the keg in the kitchen, laughing. Julia was sitting next to David, leaning against his shoulder. She looked great, of course, like she spent her days sailing and horseback riding. But she was eating her way through an impressively big bowl of salt and vinegar chips. I was surprised—I thought she ate only boring green salads, and for some reason it made me uncomfortable. I looked away before she could notice me and feel obliged to say hello. I hoped she wouldn't rat me out.

Laura and two of her friends were in the corner whispering. I flattened myself against the wall, trying to get by a couple making out.

"I'm gonna wander," I told Mouse and Nicholas.

Mouse looked worried. "Are you okay?"

"I'm fine, don't worry about me."

"I'm not letting you drink tonight."

I sighed. She was just trying to be a good friend, but I needed some space to not be Ash right now.

"They have beer," I pointed out to reassure her. "I hate beer."

"What kind of beer? Some of those companies don't have fair hiring practices," Mouse said, storming off into the kitchen to investigate. Nicholas trailed behind her, and I took the opportunity to let the crowd swallow me up. Seth was nowhere to be seen. There were only a few people dancing; some were already drunkenly flailing about, and some just wanted the excuse to press up against each other. My eardrums felt like water balloons about to pop. Whoever was in charge of the sound system had gone way overboard.

"Oh, my God. They just let anyone in to these parties," Laura said snidely.

"Are you kidding me with this shit? Seriously." I shook my head, unimpressed, before pushing past her to go upstairs where I could breathe. Laura grabbed my arm. I narrowed my eyes at her. If she'd been glass, she would have cracked clean down the middle.

"Stay away from Seth." Her fingers dug into my arm.

"Give me a break." I shook her off.

"I mean it, you little freak. I will make your life a living hell." She smiled, all teeth and temper. "You don't actually think he likes you, do you? You're this, like, scruffy little nobody."

"Well, since he dumped you, he doesn't like you either." I turned around and walked up the stairs.

"You can't go up there," Laura shouted.

"Bite me." It wasn't exactly original, but it shut her up.

The upstairs hallway was nearly dark, a single Tiffany lamp lit on a table under an open window. I leaned against the wall and closed my eyes for a moment. I was angry and tired and sad. What on earth had made me think a party would help?

"Hey."

Apparently, it might help after all. I cracked one eye open. Seth was leaning against the wall next to me, smiling that easy smile.

"Hey."

We didn't say anything else. He just leaned in and covered my mouth with his. It took my breath away. Then he kicked open the door to Jackson's sister's room behind him and pulled me inside.

We tumbled onto the bed. His body covered mine. We kissed longer, deeper, and when his hand moved under my shirt, I didn't stop him. His warm palm brushed against my belly and then higher. When we kissed like this, I knew he wasn't thinking of anyone else but me. And I liked the feeling. A lot.

But when his hand brushed the snap of my pants, I stilled.

"Seth," I said against his lip. I shook my head. "Not yet."

I woke up the next morning and pushed the bathroom door open, intent on toothpaste. Julia jumped, startled. She seemed to relax slightly when she realized it was just me. She wiped her mouth quickly and held her arm behind her back as if she was hiding something. It crinkled like a chip bag.

"Are you okay?"

She nodded. She was wearing a frilly skirt and a short-sleeved blouse. To hang around the house. She was sixteen, not forty. The girl needed to unclench. If we'd been friends, I'd have begged her to put on a pair of ripped jeans.

"I'm fine." She hurried back to her room. I swear I smelled salt and vinegar chips. Weird.

After getting dressed, I sat on my bed for way too long with a dorky smile on my face that I just couldn't seem to erase. There was no way Seth could pretend yesterday hadn't happened. We were now kissing on an almost-regular basis. Okay, twice. But last night had been for a long time, so it had to count for more than just one kiss.

When I got to the kitchen, Dad's famous chocolate-chip pancakes were all gone. Dad's mouth tightened when he saw me.

"Do you know what it's like to find your daughter's bed empty when she's supposed to be in it?"

"I'm sorry I snuck out." That, at least, was easy to apologize for. I'd actually done it and with full knowledge of the ramifications.

"You're going to do all of Katie's chores until she's better. As well as the vacuuming you've been neglecting."

I looked up. I opened my mouth to protest and then closed it again. Something in his expression made me think twice. "Fine."

"And you're still grounded until further notice. I expect better from you, Ash. Look at Julia. She's always helpful and polite. She doesn't have tantrums."

The comparisons were starting already. Great. And apparently the mysterious glass episode was being classified as a tantrum. I shoved my chair back.

"Are we done?" I asked, storming out of the kitchen before he could even reply. "Forget breakfast. I have homework."

I spotted Seth in the parking lot Monday morning. Even though he looked right at me, he ducked into the school without saying anything, without even waving.

I waited by his locker at lunch. He looked around, as if checking the hallway for familiar faces. When he didn't see any, he stopped and asked, "What's up?"

I shrugged, feeling tired and stupid for waiting when he looked like he wanted to be anywhere but here with me. I'd really thought being at the party together had made a difference. Of course, we'd been making out in a dark room, hardly hanging out where everyone could see us. He glanced over his shoulder again. I made a sound of frustration.

"Are you looking for someone?" I asked bluntly.

He turned back to face me. "Just want to make sure my friends aren't here."

"Why?"

He took my hand, kissed the back of it and led me around the corner into an empty classroom. "I told you. I don't want you to have to deal with their crap," he explained when we were alone.

I crossed my arms. "What am I, a social leper?"

He shook his head and gave me that lopsided grin that made my heart trip a little. His hand moved up my arm, his thumb just barely brushing the side of my breast.

"Well, you don't exactly fit in with the popular crowd."

"I like it that way," I pointed out archly. "And by the way, the only crowd the populars are popular with are themselves."

"Let's not fight about this, Ash." He kissed my neck while

I decided whether or not I wanted to punch him. "We just come from different groups. It's not a big deal unless you make it one."

"Don't blame me because you're being lame." It sounded strong when I said it, but I was so tired; and when he kissed me like that it drove everything out of my head. I really liked that about his kisses. I stayed in his arms until the bell rang for class. When students started to file in, he jumped away from me like I was all sharp edges.

He had no idea.

To make matters worse, Mr. Batra stopped me in the hallway.

"Ash, I'd like to speak to you."

I blinked. "Oh. Um, I have class."

"This will only take a moment." He looked at me with the kind of disappointment that adults must practise in the mirror. "I've heard you're not taking your detention very seriously."

"What?" I burst out. "I've been to all the meetings."

"Yes, but apparently you've been goofing off."

I opened my eyes wide.

"That's not true!" And it was deeply unfair. I'd already seen enough tissue paper and construction paper to last me a lifetime. "Who said that? It's a total lie."

He frowned. "I can't say who spoke to me. It wouldn't be fair."

"Fair?" I nearly stomped my foot, I was so frustrated. "What's fair about this? You're taking someone's word over mine without any proof."

"All right, Miss Perrault. No need for dramatics." He straightened his horrible tie. "And I suppose you have a point. Just make sure you work hard from now on. I want to see results."

I nodded. "Yes, Mr. Batra."

"Go on to class now."

Laura was waiting in the stairwell, watching us. She glared at me. It didn't take a genius to figure out who was behind the tattle-telling.

I glared back and marched past her down the stairs to the art room. Mr. Batra wanted proof? Laura wanted me out of her way? Fine.

Ms. Harding was sitting behind her desk. The class was only half full. Everyone was busy working on projects. I walked right up to her. She looked up, startled.

"Hello, Ash."

"Hi. Um, do you have a minute?"

"Sure."

I bit my lower lip. The plan was only half-formed in my head. What if she laughed at me?

"It's about the mosaics."

"Oh, yes. I meant to tell you I really liked that plate you made. You have a knack for it."

"Thanks. I never thought I'd get so into it, you know? I'm even covering my fireplace. It's a little messy on the bottom where I first started, but I think it'll turn out okay." I took a deep breath. "Um, I don't know if you know, but I have detention."

She pursed her lips.

"Because of the mural. Yes, I know."

Oops. I'd forgotten that as an art teacher she might have taken that personally.

"Oh, right. Well, Mr. Batra wants to know that I'm really working as part of the dance committee. Anyway, I was wondering if I could do a big mosaic somewhere. Kind of like the mural."

She looked at me for a long moment before nodding. "I don't see why not."

The air left my lungs in a rush. "Really?" *So there, Laura, you sneaky cow. Two can play this game. I'll work so hard Mr. Batra will sing my praises.* "Um, could it be someplace obvious?"

"I'll speak to Mr. Batra," Ms. Harding continued. "I've wanted to do something about that hinged wooden panel that hides props and the stairs leading to the stage in the auditorium for years now. You know the one?"

"Yeah." It was usually covered in half-assed graffiti and old chewing gum.

"It's ugly, Ash."

I had to grin. "It really is," I echoed.

"Good." She pushed her glasses back up her nose. "Then it's settled."

I had to wait a few days before I had a chance to sneak out to Mouse's. And even then, it was only because I had a spare and had got off early. Mouse was working on the half-finished piece currently spilling out of Ariadne's metal-toothed maw. I wasn't sure what it was. It looked like a cross between a flapper dress and a wedding sari. It was beautiful material, and I had no doubt that whatever Mouse was creating would end up looking just right on her. She could pull anything off.

"What happened with Seth?" Mouse asked me finally. I knew she didn't like him, so it was nice of her not to sneer.

I stared at the ceiling, remembering the way he'd touched my cheek.

"It was nice. He's so cute."

"Anything happen?"

"Not really," I hedged.

Mouse concentrated on cutting the fabric. "Not really? Does that mean yes?" she asked around the pins in her mouth.

I shrugged, fighting a goofy grin. "He kissed me. A lot."

The pins fell on the carpet. I could tell she was already

contemplating how to best hold a demonstration and picket my choice in crushes. "Really?" she said instead. "Again? How was it?"

"It was great." I fiddled with the ring on my thumb. "Really great."

"Oh." Mouse kept cutting. The squeak and snap of the scissors was comforting. "Hold this down, would you?" she asked. I crouched down and helped her manoeuvre the fabric. I really didn't want to talk about Seth anymore.

"Thanks for not trying to convince me to dress up as a Greenpeace banner or something."

"I would never push my opinions on another person." Her eyes twinkled.

"Of course you wouldn't."

Katie loved that I had to do all of her chores. She sat and ate a Popsicle, letting it drip all over the kitchen table I'd just wiped down.

"Bring me a yogurt," she said.

I shoved one at her.

"Not that kind. The one with fruit already mixed in."

I shot her a look. "I may have to do your chores, but I'm not your servant. Get your own yogurt."

"Then get started cleaning my room," she smirked. "That's one of my chores."

"I didn't throw that damned glass at you," I muttered, "but I'm beginning to wish I had."

I stomped into her bedroom, and she hobbled after me. She lay on her bed and proceeded to tell me exactly where all of her things had to go. She even had me dust her desk. Hello? They'd barely moved in; there hadn't been time for any dust to accumulate. I rearranged her CDs so they were easier to reach and handed her the phone when it rang. She waved me away like I was a servant.

I really wanted to shove one of her Hello Kitty erasers up her nose.

Instead, I went into my room and spent the next hour making more sketches for the school mosaic. I thought it might be nice to do some kind of forest scene, lots of autumn leaves and a stormy sunset sky. But it might be boring. Should I do something more fun? Maybe something for Halloween, with vampires and pumpkins and black cats? I couldn't decide.

If I waited much longer I'd have to go with Mouse's idea of a parade of beheaded queens, each holding her own head under her arm.

I flipped through the mosaic book for ideas. I made a sketch, hated it. Made another one, hated it too. The design for the fireplace had come so quickly to me. I balled up my sketches and tossed them at the garbage. They missed, and I had to get up to throw them out properly. As I did, I noticed a nest of crumpled chip bags and chocolate bar wrappers in my garbage. I frowned. I hadn't thrown those out.

I remembered Julia eating chips in the bathroom. I frowned harder. It wouldn't be like her to hide garbage or try and get me into trouble.

It was more like Katie. She must have been hiding this stuff under my garbage so Ella wouldn't find out she was sneaking snacks.

I opened the bathroom door. "Katie, stay out of my room!" I hollered. The tiles made the sound echo. "Use your own damn garbage."

"Katie's not here. She went out with Mom and your dad."

Julia sat up from where she'd been reading on her bed while Katie and I squabbled. Her smile seemed cautious, and she wasn't meeting my eyes. She was probably afraid I was going to freak out on her.

I dumped the handfuls of empty snack wrappers on the floor.

"Well, tell her if she sneaks into my room again, I'll tell your mom she's been scarfing all that junk food."

"Don't worry. I'll tell her. Sorry."

I shrugged bad-temperedly. "It's not your fault."

I tried not to think about how Katie was out with my dad who had barely spoken to me all week.

I decided to hide out at Mouse's for the rest of the day. I was spending a lot of time there, when I wasn't sweeping or dusting or trying not to commit stepsister murder. I pushed open the door to Mouse's room.

"Hey, your mom let me—whoa!" I froze, my mouth hanging open. I said the first thing that popped into my head. "My eyes!"

Nicholas scrambled off the bed where he'd been sprawled on top of Mouse. On top of Mouse! His hair was dishevelled. When Mouse sat up, blushing, her shirt was half-unbuttoned. I didn't know where to look.

"What?" I sputtered. I might have made a coherent sentence, but I'd forgotten how.

Nicholas dragged his hand through his air, his eyes never leaving his shoes.

"I should go," he gulped, before grabbing his jacket and rushing past me. "Bye, Ash."

"Coward," Mouse muttered.

I sat down hard on the nearest chair even though it was covered in bolts of fabric.

"I don't get it," I said. "You and Nicholas?"

Mouse nodded.

"Since when?"

"It kind of just happened over the last couple of weeks."

I stared at her, hurt. "Why didn't you tell me?"

She looked away, looked back. "I don't know. You've had

so much going on," she said quietly. "You've been kind of cranky."

"Oh." I didn't know what else to say. My best friends were going out now? "Oh," I repeated. "Okay."

Mouse seemed to deflate in front of my eyes with relief. "Yeah?" she said. "Cool."

We just sat there for a minute staring at each other. I'd never been awkward with Mouse before. It was awful.

"Did he ask you to the dance?" I asked, already knowing the answer.

"We'll all go together."

"Nah." I tried to sound casual.

Question: what would be worse than not having Seth actually ask me? Answer: tagging along with my best friend and her date.

Because of all the chores I have to do now, I swear I live in the kitchen.

In some stories, there would be talking mice or a wise old dog helping me. In real life, if there were mice, I'd have to sweep up after them.

Dad will have to get a cleaning lady.

If he thinks I'm going to do this forever, he's crazy.

CHAPTER 6

When I got home, Ella was in the kitchen with Julia. I could hear them laughing. I tried to tiptoe past the door toward my bedroom, but Ella saw me.

"Hello, Ash. Want to see some of the dress options?"

"I have a lot of homework to do." I couldn't think of anything more boring than looking at puffy white dresses. The table was covered in bridal magazines.

"Isn't this one beautiful?" Ella pointed to a dress that looked like a meringue.

I paused. "Seriously?"

"Hah!" Julia said. "I told you it was awful." She looked at

me triumphantly. "Thank you."

"Okay," I said.

Ella flipped through another magazine and showed me a folded page. "Julia and Katie will wear this for a bridesmaid's dress. Cute, don't you think?"

Silence.

"Well, what do you think, Ash?" Julia asked.

It was red and would clash horribly with my hair. Not that I'd been asked, because I hadn't, and not that I wanted to be a bridesmaid, because I didn't. But I also didn't want to be the only family member left out of the wedding party.

"Um, nice. I gotta get to my homework."

"Oh, Ash," Ella said, as if she was remembering something important.

I paused mid-escape. "Yeah?"

"Make sure you ask us before you mosaic any more of the house, okay?"

I just blinked at her. "What? Dad said I could."

She smiled gently. "I know, and you do beautiful work. You really do. But if there's too much of it, and we ever want to sell the house and move, we won't be able to."

"Dad said I could," I repeated lamely. I didn't know what else to say. I wasn't taking down the fireplace mosaic. I hadn't even finished it yet.

"I know, but he agrees with me. So does the real estate agent."

Whoa.

"Are we moving?" I asked, suddenly suspicious.

She shook her head. "Of course not. But we'd like to keep our options open."

"What about the fireplace?" I didn't know why I asked. I had no intention of listening to her if she wanted me to take it apart.

"The fireplace is fine. I'm just saying for next time. Though now that we're on the topic, make sure it's all cleaned up in there for the party tomorrow, okay?"

"Fine," I snapped and went to my room, slamming the door behind me.

That was just what I needed, a boring cocktail party full of boring adults who would ask me how school was and if I had a boyfriend.

And worse, the stupid party was on my *birthday.*

In the morning, I was hoping for chocolate-chip pancakes or hot chocolate or something. There was just the regular cereal and juice, but Dad said he would drive me to school. On our way out, Ella glanced over at what I was wearing.

"Oh, Ash, there's a hole in your shirt."

"I know."

It was my favourite T-shirt, all thin and soft. It was fraying slightly at the hem, and there was a hole in the back near the collar. The hole was tiny, barely the size of a dime.

"Shouldn't you change it? What if they send you home?"

"They're not going to send me home," I said. "They never do that."

"I have a lovely blouse. It's brand new. You could wear it if you'd like. Or borrow something from Julia."

Dad smiled. "See that? New clothes!"

Had Dad gone nuts? Since when were new clothes a reward in my world?

"And you do look a little rumpled, pumpkin."

I rolled my eyes. "I'll be late," I mumbled before dashing out to the car. There was no way I would change my shirt.

Dad hadn't driven me to school in months, maybe he was about to give me a really kick-ass present. Like a new computer. Okay, maybe not. But he'd given Katie a cellphone, so I was bound to get something at least as good as that. Maybe, finally, a television for my room?

"I want to talk to you, budgie."

Or not.

"Okay," I kept my face turned to the window, watching the neighbourhood become a blur.

"Ash, what's going on with you these days? You're sullen and unpleasant."

My stomach felt like it was full of glue. He hadn't even wished me a happy birthday.

He pulled the car over to the curb, across from the high

school. I traced the fall of a raindrop on the glass with my finger. I wondered if there'd be a crack following the path of my fingertip. Nothing. I pressed harder. Still nothing. I dropped my hand in my lap and willed the window to move, crack, shatter—anything.

"I want you to be the nice girl I know and love for the engagement party tonight."

"And that's it? That's all you have to say to me?"

He had no idea it was my birthday. He'd forgotten—no doubt because I wasn't the *nice* girl he loved. I jumped out of the car and slammed the door behind me.

Inside, the bell was already ringing and the halls were packed. I shoved past people, ignoring their annoyed glares. I hit someone hard with my shoulder and didn't care. I didn't even look back. When a hand grabbed my arm, I nearly snarled.

I was yanked into a dark utility closet. The door clicked shut and I was in shadows, propped between a broom and a mop.

"What the hell?"

The hallway light seeped through the edges of the door, showing me Seth's smile. I really hoped he couldn't see that I'd been crying. I didn't want to get into it. I didn't want to be the messed-up girl with a bad attitude. I just wanted to be the girl who got kissed in the dark.

I grabbed him before he could say anything and kissed

him hard. I lost myself in the kiss. I didn't want to be Ash Perrault for a second longer. Anyone else would do.

Mouse and Nicholas were sitting together at lunchtime. It wasn't unusual, but it just felt different this time. They were holding hands and smiling. When I passed Seth's table, he caught my eye. I nearly blushed, remembering how he'd grabbed me. I hadn't even told him it was my birthday. He winked at me, but he didn't wave me over to his table. I thought Laura might have caught the wink. She certainly glowered at me like I was something squishy she'd just found under her shoe. She whispered something to Michelle, who looked at me and laughed. Subtle.

I stopped at Mouse and Nicholas' table.

"Happy birthday!" Mouse all but shouted. Heads turned toward us. She ignored them and pulled a small Tupperware container out of her bag.

"Here. Sit and eat."

I pulled the top off to find a chocolate cupcake with pink and purple sprinkles to match my hair. For some reason, it made me want to cry. My smile was definitely wobbly.

"Thanks, Mouse."

"'Course."

Nicholas nudged my hip. "Aren't you going to sit? I'm getting a crick in my neck."

"Nah, I'm gonna go measure the panel for my project. I've only got what, two weeks? I'm going to have to come in on the weekend as it is."

Mouse narrowed her eyes at me. "Are you okay?"

I tried to make my smile less wobbly. "Sure, I just want to get the design figured out. Thanks for the cupcake."

I fled to the auditorium.

It felt weird to go off and sit alone in a corner, but I wasn't in the mood to pretend it was normal for my best friends to be pawing at each other. Or that it was normal for the guy I was making out with often enough to know he chewed spearmint gum, to pretend he didn't see me.

All in all, I just wanted to be left alone to feel sorry for myself. And I really did have to sketch this design before the next bell. Students in three of Ms. Harding's art classes were supposed to snip and cut tiles and break old plates for me today and she needed to know colours and quantity.

I couldn't make it too complicated. I didn't have the time, and plus I didn't think I had enough experience to pull off some detailed Roman frieze. I thought about doing a big sunflower or lots of little stars or autumn leaves on a blue-sky background.

In the end I decided I'd make my own version of the comedy and tragedy masks since it was a panel mostly used by drama classes. I'd never liked the traditional masks. They were kind of creepy. Instead, I sketched out half-masks, like they used to wear at masquerade balls in the eighteenth century. And then I wove in the Harvest Queen and King theme into them as well. One of the masks would be the queen with a little crown and berries dangling from the edges. The eyes would be sad. I'd make the other face the king, also with a crown but this one mostly made of autumn leaves. Everything else would be simple tiles all in blue, the way the sky looked on clear October mornings.

I still had the auditorium to myself after lunch, so I stayed there for my spare. I took a short break from sketching and lined up three empty juice bottles on one of the tables. I sat on a chair a good six feet from the table and crossed my legs, the way people did when they meditated or did yoga. I stared really hard at the first bottle, so hard that my eyes watered. There was a dull throb of a headache brewing behind my forehead. Even my shoulders were tight, ready to snap like an overstretched elastic band.

But I kept staring. And staring.

And when I got annoyed and started to feel like a complete idiot, and so frustrated I was on the verge of tears, the bottles exploded. It was like frozen rain scattering across the table and the floor and over my legs. Even the tiles piled in the bucket under my mosaic shivered. I ducked, covering my head. One of the bottles hadn't actually exploded; it was just cracked. I got up and marched right up to it.

"I am frustrated," I announced out loud.

Nothing happened. But I knew, I just knew in my bones, that I was on to something. I leaned over, an inch from the bottle.

"I said," I ground out between my teeth, remembering all of those other incidents when glass broke even though I never intended it to. "I am frustrated."

I thought about my mosaics, all those broken shards with veins of grout running between them. I pictured the bottle veined in that same way, tracing the frozen rivers and releasing them. The crack deepened and a piece flew off and nearly took my eye out. It skittered under a table. It was sharp enough to draw blood.

I used my sketchpad to sweep the broken glass into the bucket. I swallowed and decided to do something safer, like working on my mosaic. I could really hurt someone if I kept this up.

I missed the bus. And then while I waited for the next one, it started to rain. It wasn't just a bad day. It was a bad day in a bad week in a bad month in a bad year. I mean, seriously, how much was I expected to put up with? And now, to top it all off, I was late for the stupid cocktail party. When the bus didn't slow down at my stop, I yanked the bell viciously. When the bus driver finally let me out, the window in the door cracked, spreading like a spider's web dipped in glitter.

"Hey!" the driver exclaimed. But he didn't say anything else. I hadn't kicked it or shoved it. I hadn't even touched it. I didn't look up, just trudged along the sidewalk. A streetlamp at the corner of the block blew into pieces. When I reached the shards, I stepped over them and kept walking.

I probably should have been frightened, but I just felt tired. Of myself, of my circumstances, of the whole damn everything. If my dad were here he'd give me that scared who-are-you look. The one I hated even more than the I'm-disappointed-in-you look. At least it was hard for him not to notice me then.

The windshield of the neighbour's car was already cracked, had been for months. But when I glared at it, the glass scattered everywhere like stars falling out of the sky. It glittered in the grass and over the pavement. I swear something broke inside me too. I was filled with the sound of glass breaking. Nothing else.

When the alarm under the dash went off, wailing into the twilight, I ran inside. I had visions of police cars driving up the street. I hurried into the front hall, where a woman in a white buttoned-down shirt and tie bustled by, smiling at me politely. She held a tray of canapés.

"Is that the neighbour's car alarm again? I thought he got it fixed." Dad poked his head out of the kitchen, looking decidedly frazzled. "Never mind, there's no time. You're late."

"Dad. It's my—"

He pointed his finger at me. "No," he said grimly. "Go get ready. The guests will be here any minute."

I slunk by him to my bedroom. I yanked a skirt out of the back of my closet. It had flowers all over it. It was most definitely not my style. But perfect for tonight. There was a white shirt hanging over my desk chair. It wasn't really my style either, with lace and beading. Ella must have put it there.

Maybe not-my-style was a good thing. Because clearly my style wasn't working for me lately.

The party was nearly as awful as I'd thought it would be.

There was a fire burning in the fireplace and tall white taper candles everywhere. There were baskets of bread and crackers and wheels of cheese. There were tiny spinach pies, olive tapenade, little cherry tarts, grapes, pâté and fresh strawberries.

I stood by the fireplace with a stupid smile plastered on my face wearing stupid pantyhose and uncomfortable shoes. I answered every question very politely. Julia was doing the same thing on the other side of the room, only she seemed actually interested in what people were saying to her. Katie leaned on her crutches, which she had decorated with a glitter pen. I had to run and fetch her ginger ale whenever she misplaced it or decided it was too far to retrieve with her aching ankle. Everyone thought it was so nice how helpful I was with my younger stepsister.

There wasn't a single birthday balloon, a single cupcake with a candle, a single present wrapped in silver paper. Nothing.

Andy came up to me and tipped his champagne flute against my glass of ginger ale. He was my dad's oldest friend. They watched football games together and swore at the television, and he always gave me money for my birthday. He'd been one of the pallbearers at my mom's funeral.

"Cheers."

I smiled another smile. "Hi, Andy. Nice tie."

He hugged me. "How's it going?"

"I'm fine." I almost added, *It's my birthday.* But I changed my mind. "I'm fine," I repeated.

"Are you going to make a toast?"

I stared at him in horror. He winked.

"No?"

I shook my head.

"Well, I guess I'd better then."

He cleared his throat.

"Excuse me," he called over the din of voices. "Excuse me, everyone." He lifted his glass as the conversation faded and all eyes turned to him. "I'd like to make a toast."

Glasses were held up dutifully. I stood in the corner next

to the antique mirror. "I've known Douglas for a long time, since he stole my baseball cards when we were seven."

"I remember that differently," my dad called out laughing.

Andy waved him away. "As I was saying, I've known Douglas a long time. After Kim died, he made it his business to be the best dad out there, and I think, seeing his beautiful and talented daughter tonight, you can all agree he did a fine job. And since meeting Ella, Douglas has had a twinkle in his eye again. She's made him so happy, in fact, that he's going to lend me his convertible and not shoot me when I return it with a tiny little scratch."

There was a ripple of laughter. "To Ella, who has given Douglas all the happiness he deserves. To Douglas, for not letting it get away. To the happy couple!"

"To the happy couple!" everyone chorused.

Dad and Ella kissed. Watching them, I realized Andy was right. Dad was happier than I'd seen him in a long time.

I didn't want to look, so I stared at the vase of roses next to me. It shattered, scattering shards of glass across the floor and half the buffet table. There were several gasps and then dead silence.

Dad pushed through the crowd and grabbed my elbow.

"Outside, young lady."

"Dad…"

"*Now.*"

He all but dragged me out onto the porch, Ella close behind. He was red in the face. Sparrows landed in the backyard tree, watching us through the glass. I thought about Mom's birds on the windowsill and shivered.

I blinked back tears. "I didn't touch it."

"So it just fell apart on its own? Come on, Ash. That wasn't clumsiness; it was deliberate. I just don't know what to do with you," he said in disgust.

"She needs a little time," Ella said. "I had a stepmother too," she added. "I don't want to be your mother, Ash, just your friend."

"Then why did you get rid of my mother's bowl?" I had no idea why I even brought it up. It just sort of rushed out of my mouth before I could stop myself. A sparrow beat itself against its own reflection in the glass of the porch door, all beak and frantic wings.

They both blinked at me.

"Oh, Ash, it's not like that. I had no idea..." He ran his hand through his hair. "I was afraid it would...get broken," he added very softly.

I felt cold all over. I didn't need him to explain what he meant.

"I know it's hard for you, but I hope you can see how happy we are," Ella murmured, misreading me completely. "I could never take your father from you. It's just not possible."

Dad nodded. "That's not the way love works, Ash. My heart has more room in it than you think."

Leaving aside the fact that it was the corniest thing he'd ever said, it also wasn't true. If it was, we wouldn't be fighting in furious whispers while dozens of guests ate shrimp in the next room.

I looked him straight in the eye. "What's today, Dad?"

He looked confused.

"What?"

I shook my head.

"It's my birthday."

I didn't say anything else. I just turned and walked away.

I left the house before anyone else was even awake. I didn't want to have to see anyone, so I went to school, which was nearly empty, it being Saturday. The janitorial staff was there and Mr. Batra, talking on the phone in his office. I gathered the smalti and glue and grout from the art room and went and stood in front of the panel. I put my earphones on and cranked the music as loud as I could stand it.

I spent the next few hours gluing bits of blue tile as the background. It was simple, all lines across until you reached the images in the centre. One of my books had called it *opus tessellatum*. They had all these different names for mosaic techniques in ancient Rome. That was the only one I knew.

I felt light-headed, like there wasn't enough air in the room. Like I didn't exist.

I hardly knew myself anymore, only knew that everyone else in the entire universe seemed to have an easier life than I did.

Julia didn't seem to have much trouble adjusting to her new life. Not that I wanted to look like her or anything. I didn't want the carbon-copy perky look. I liked my tattered tank tops and cargo pants, and I liked it even more that I never had to think about what to wear or if my lipstick clashed. Way too much effort. But I couldn't deny everything seemed to go smoothly for Ella and Julia and Katie, with their brushed hair and ironed shirts. Everyone liked them— especially my father. He couldn't stop raving about Julia's grades and Julia's manners.

But he wasn't raving about me much at all these days.

And clearly, neither was Seth.

I was just going to have to stop. I was going to have to be happy and calm and blend in. I was not going to be a freak anymore. Because Dad was right, I could have broken Mom's bowl.

The big hair, the perfect make-up, the graceful entrance—Princess or Prom Queen, they have it down. Those twelve dancing princess could spin gracefully all night long, and they were smart enough to hide their tracks. And there are always midnight balls and silver crowns and princes that turn into bears or out of bears, depending on what kind of night it is. .

A ball might be cool, but a high school dance? Not so much. It's all petty fights, boys hiding beer and girls crying in the washroom. And there's always that perfect couple wrapped around each other—perfect dress and perfect hair and perfect kisses. Perfect princess moment.

Hardly.

CHAPTER 7

On Monday morning, I dressed carefully. If I wasn't going to be Ash anymore, I had to start somewhere. I put on a skirt and the white shirt Ella had left for me. I thought I should do something about my pink and purple hair, but that would have to wait. For now I pulled it back in a ponytail with one of Julia's ribbons. It was just barely long enough. I didn't talk to anyone over breakfast, but no one noticed my new look. Everyone was rushing around trying not to be late.

I walked to school even though it was damp and cold. I just wanted to be alone. The trees lining the sidewalk scattered raindrops and red leaves over my head. I paid attention in all of my classes and handed in my homework, which I'd dutifully finished on Sunday. At lunch I stood in front of the mosaic and frowned. A huge piece of it was missing and tiny tiles lay on the floor, broken. Fixing it would set me back at least a couple of hours.

I really hoped I hadn't done that. I remembered the car windows, the vases. I folded my arms in front of my chest, hunching my shoulders slightly. I wasn't going to be that girl anymore, I reminded myself sternly.

Seth walked by me in his dark jeans and a tight T-shirt. His arms looked slender and strong as oak branches.

"Nice shirt," he murmured.

On Tuesday, I walked to school again and didn't talk to a single person. I saw Laura giggling with Jackson in the hallway. He nuzzled her neck. I hoped that meant she was over Seth and would finally get off my case. I was happy for her. And even happier for myself.

Not so happy, however, to see Seth standing in a classroom doorway watching them and glowering. He didn't notice me; he was too busy scowling.

After that, I avoided everyone, spent lunch in the library with my math homework and stayed after school to work on my project.

I came home after dinner, cleaned up the dirty dishes and ate leftovers in my room and then did Katie's chore: cleaning the bathroom. Dad and Ella went to a movie. Julia studied. Katie watched movies and talked to her friends online.

I broke a vase by accident. No one saw. I put all the bits of glass into the recycling box. It was only one little vase. It didn't mean anything.

On Wednesday, Mouse cornered me in the hallway. She was wearing a twenties cloche hat and ripped jeans. Somehow, it didn't look weird on her. I was wearing pantyhose under my skirt.

"What the hell are those?" she asked, pointing at them as if they were made of endangered baby seals.

"Pantyhose."

She raised an eyebrow. "Pantyhose? What are you, forty?"

"Laundry day," I said, because it was easier.

"Let me sew for you, I'm begging you."

"No way."

"Ash, where have you been anyway?"

I looked up after dumping my books in my locker.

"What?"

"Earth to Ash. You've been spacey all week."

"Sorry. I've just been really busy. I don't have much time to finish that mosaic."

Mouse took a cookie out of her bag. It was wrapped in plastic and stuffed with raisins and what looked like dates. She made a face. "Nicholas is making me eat weird healthy things," she complained.

I had to smile. "He's always done that."

"He's always tried. Now, I'm actually letting him." She shuddered playfully. "Scary."

I slung my knapsack over my shoulder as she took a bite, chewed, made a face and wrapped the cookie up again.

"Note to self," she said. "Just say no to wheat germ." She shoved it back in her bag, glancing over her shoulder to make sure Nicholas wasn't around to see her. "So you need help with the mosaic?"

I wanted to say yes. The old Ash would have said yes. But I didn't want to hear Mouse go on about my trendy dull clothes or how Seth wasn't my type or how different I was now. I didn't want to agree with her. The new Ash shook her head.

"No thanks."

On my way home, I stopped at the drugstore. I ignored my usual brand of hair dye and went straight to one with a blondish looking girl with a big smile.

On Thursday, I went to school with my normal hair colour, which I hadn't seen in two years. It looked like weak tea.

Seth walked right by me before he even recognized who I was.

"Ash." He raised his eyebrows. "Nice."

He even said it in front of Noah. I tried not to smile all the way to class.

Later, I found more broken pieces of tile on the floor in front of my project, scattered like multicoloured dust. It didn't make sense. Mosaics calmed me; I wasn't frustrated and angry when I worked on them, so I couldn't be doing it. I was beginning to think I was losing my mind.

That night, we had dinner as a family. Ella offered me potatoes and I said thank you. Katie dropped her fork smeared in gravy on my knee and I didn't say anything, and even though I wanted to stick peas up her nose, I went and got her a new fork instead. My dad smiled more than he had since Ella agreed to marry him. I could feel them exchanging a happy glance when I cleared the table without being asked.

Dad gave me a small TV for my room as a belated birthday present.

On Friday, Seth asked me to sit with him and his friends at lunch. It was definitely a step up from dark parks and dusty closets. It was the first time we had been seen in public together, and I could feel the whispers coursing through the room. Seth laughed with Noah over some movie they'd seen the night before. Mouse and Nicholas sat at the next table and scowled at us. Seth reached for my hand, and I forgot everything else.

Sophie told me she liked the way I'd done my hair, in a sleek bob. It wasn't that different from my old hair, just brushed and not the colour of cotton candy. I smiled. Even though I missed my carnival hair, it was kind of nice sitting there.

Laura brought her tray to the table, pausing.

"Excuse me?" she said icily. "What is she doing here?"

An awkward silence descended.

"Laura, don't," Julia said quietly.

Seth didn't say anything at all.

"Whatever," Laura sniffed, sitting down and glaring at me.

I ignored her and pushed my sandwich around on my plate. I'd hoped Seth would at least say something, anything, about Laura being rude to me, but he wouldn't even look at me. Still, at least we weren't hiding anymore. Then the bell rang and he leaned over and kissed me quickly, in front of God and the whole school. When he glanced over at Laura, she choked on her granola bar.

I felt like a princess.

Even if the prince *had* looked at his ex-girlfriend after our first public kiss instead of at me.

Saturday night, I opened my eyes, wondering what had woken me up. I could only hear the wind in the trees. The streetlights were still on, making my curtains glow. I turned over and closed my eyes.

Which was when I heard the sound again, faintly. I sat up, listening, until I realized it was coming from the adjoining bathroom. Someone was sick and crying.

I kicked free of my blankets. As much as Katie got on my nerves, I couldn't just leave her alone. Maybe her foot really was still hurting. I eased the door open, about to offer to go and get Ella, when I realized the person sprawled on the cold tiles and gripping the toilet wasn't Katie. It was Julia, and she hadn't heard me yet. Her face was white. She stood up and wiped her mouth with a towel.

I eased behind the door, feeling uncertain. I should probably say something. But what? I opened the door again. I hated this.

Julia was now at the sink brushing her teeth. Her eyes were red.

"Um," I said.

She jumped, looking guilty.

"Are you okay?" I asked. My voice felt creaky.

She smiled. "Sure." She tossed her toothbrush back into the plastic cup. The bristles were worn down.

"Are you sure?"

Her smile didn't waver. "I'm okay. I just have a little

119

PMS. Good night."

She didn't even look back, just rushed into her room.

Frowning, I climbed into my bed, but it took me a long time to fall asleep.

Dad and Ella were snuggling over French toast the next morning when I got up. They were so into each other that Dad hadn't even noticed Grimm lounging on the kitchen counter in a patch of sunlight. Katie was slurping her chocolate milk, and Julia was eating a slice of cantaloupe in perfect tiny bites with a knife and fork. She wouldn't look me in the eye.

"Morning, budgie," Dad said, glancing over.

I was always miserable in the morning. Even before Dad's speeches on attitude adjustments, and even with the natural hair colour and skirts.

"Would you like some breakfast?" Ella asked. "There's lots left."

I shook my head and mumbled something into my coffee cup. There were still roses in crystal bowls all over the house left over from the party. The scent was strong, cloying. Some of the petals were wilting.

"There's a bridal show in town today," Dad said.

Ella smiled at him. "There are so many details to plan. July will be here before we know it."

A summer vacation spent with caterers and wedding photographers loomed before me. Not that it mattered. I wasn't in the wedding party anyway.

"Julia's going to be the maid of honour," Katie said around a mouthful of French toast. Her foot was propped up on a chair, looking normal.

"We'd like it if you came along with us today," Dad said cheerfully. "We'll go as a family."

Good thing I'd already swallowed my mouthful of coffee or I would have sprayed it right out my nose. Spending the morning looking at taffeta dresses sounded like hell. I agreed to go because I had come this far with being the new Ash. But I texted Mouse in the car all the way downtown.

The bridal show was in one of the big hotels. Dad and Ella couldn't possibly have thought it would be fun to haul us about gathering pamphlets for cheesy reception bands and florists and tuxedo shops. At least there was cake. I spent the better part of an hour waiting in the bakery lines to taste-test cake. The weird lemon thing was gross, but the vanilla and the chocolate were okay. I managed to avoid everyone, until I noticed Julia in one of the other bakery lines. She didn't look like she'd seen me though, so I didn't have to tense up or try and play nice. I could go back to my cake.

Come to think of it, Julia seemed to be enjoying the cake too. Enjoying it quite a bit for a girl who mostly ate lettuce.

She had three different pieces on her paper plate and they were huge. She scooped up whorls of icing, focusing steadily on her plastic fork as if there was no one else in the world. It wasn't fair. If I ate that much cake I'd probably gain twenty pounds. God, even her metabolism was perfect. And to think she envied me when I ate a chocolate bar for breakfast.

It didn't really make sense. It didn't look right either, the way she was eating. *Not my problem*, I told myself. *She's a big girl, and everyone's always saying how mature she is. I'm sure she's fine. What do I know anyway?*

A man's cheerful voice boomed over the loudspeaker to announce the start of the fashion show. I groaned. New Ash or not, if I had to sit through a fashion show I was going to need more cake too. Lots more cake. Dad found me hiding behind a fake palm tree, a scoop of candied almonds in my hand. I was probably going to get into trouble for not sitting in the front row and clapping at the tulle and lace monstrosities.

"Dad, I can't sit through a fashion show," I said, and it sounded like I was begging, even to my own ears. Ella, Julia and Katie were now sitting in a neat row, waiting expectantly for the parade of meringue dresses.

Dad winked at me.

"Those dresses scare me too," he said in a conspiratorial whisper. "I'm afraid Ella will get trapped in one and have to chew her way out."

I grinned despite myself.

"Let's wander for a bit," he suggested. The aisles were crowded, and we spotted more than one argument brewing. Dad got caught up in a veil a woman threw over her shoulder to see if it would float properly. He spat out a mouthful of tulle with such a look of dread, I had to laugh.

He gave me one of those awkward Dad-side-shoulder hugs.

"I miss that laugh," he said.

Trying to regain some composure, I quickly ran my tongue over my parched lips. I had held my smile too long and looked away, embarrassed. "I want to ask you something, budgie."

"What?" I asked suspiciously.

He laughed. "It's not about school or boys." He paused. "There isn't a boy, is there?" There was a trace of mild panic in his voice.

"Not really," I said. I had absolutely no intention of getting into the complicated mess that was Seth and me with my *father*.

"Thank God," he muttered. "Anyway, it's about the wedding. I'd like you to be my best man."

"Really?" I felt a rush of pleasure mixed with a whole bunch of other feelings I couldn't identify. "What about Andy?"

"Andy can be a flower girl with Katie." We exchanged grins. Andy would do it too, if my dad asked him. And he'd do it in drag. "Come on Ash, what do you say? I think your mother would have loved the idea."

He stood there waiting for my answer, with this goofy happy smile on his face.

"Okay," I said. "I'll be your best man."

Seth and I spent an hour filling garbage bags with leaves for the dance at the end of the week. It was a good opportunity to escape Laura and her clipboard-checklist frenzy. It might have only taken us half the time if we hadn't taken advantage of the empty field behind the school. As we lay in the long grass, I could hear the distant sounds of people playing football, traffic on the road and the birds in trees.

"We have to get back," I said, fumbling as I did up the buttons on my shirt. "They'll wonder why we've been gone so long."

He nodded and got up, holding out his hand to help me. It was kind of sweet. Why couldn't he be that sweet when other people were around? At least he wasn't afraid to be seen with me anymore. That had to count for something.

We walked back to the school, and I didn't care that I was dishevelled with bits of leaves on my clothing. Seth went on ahead when I stopped to gather a few more leaves to fill out my bag. I wasn't about to give Laura any excuse to snitch to Mr. Batra. When I went in through the side door, I saw Mouse wearing an Edwardian dress with a tattered jean jacket. She wasn't alone. I paused when she grabbed Seth's sleeve. I eased halfway behind the door so they wouldn't see me.

He blinked at her. "What?" he asked.

Mouse folded her arms. "I want to talk to you."

"I'm late."

Her gaze didn't slide away. "I don't care. What are you doing with Ash?"

I was too mortified to move or make a sound.

Seth's lip curled. "What are you, her mother?"

"No. If you paid any attention at all, you'd know Ash's mom died."

Mouse spoke through clenched teeth. I could feel the blood draining out of my face. I felt light, dizzy.

Seth looked surprised. "I didn't know Ash's mom died."

"Well, duh."

He frowned. "You got a problem, Mouse?"

"That's Victoria to you." She poked him in the chest. "And while Ash may buy that you're really into her, I have not forgotten that you were embarrassed to be seen with her not two weeks ago. And now that Laura's with someone, you're suddenly groping Ash in the hallways."

"Forget your Midol this morning?" Seth asked.

I shrank back against the bricks. I was humiliated enough as it was; I didn't want them to know I was there. Mouse looked as if she was counting to five, the way she did when she was really about to lose her temper.

"I know you were embarrassed to be seen with her because you're an idiot, but I'm warning you that if you hurt her, I will personally break both your ankles."

He shook his head. "You're bent, Piercy."

She leaned in closer. "You have no idea. Remember what I said."

Seth just walked back inside with the bags of leaves we'd gathered. I stalked up to Mouse, shaking my head.

"What the hell was that about?" I asked angrily.

She tried to smile. "Oh, uh, nothing. Just saying hi."

I'd been nice and quiet for days now. I'd swallowed every retort and smothered any layer of tone under a smothering silence. Right now, it was easier to be mad at Mouse. She was the only one who actually liked the old me better than the new and improved me. And if she liked the old Ash so much, I was afraid I'd go back to being her. I couldn't afford it. The old Ash didn't have a cute boyfriend who kissed her in the long grass and she didn't have a dad who'd asked her to be his best man.

"Why the hell did you spew all over Seth?"

Mouse looked trapped.

"I couldn't help it. He makes me mad."

"You had no right to do that. Do you have any idea how mortifying this is?"

Mouse scowled. "Is he your boyfriend now?"

I wasn't sure how to answer that. Mostly because I still didn't know.

"Why?" I asked.

"Ash, he was afraid to be seen in public with you. You can't tell me that's romantic."

"He didn't want to upset Laura. It's different now."

"Different because you're different."

I shrugged.

"So what?"

She looked at me like I'd grown another head.

"Are you kidding? Why was he more interested in the delicate sensibilities of his ex-girlfriend than his current girlfriend?"

I flushed.

"I'm not his girlfriend." I hated having to say that. Besides, it might not be true.

Mouse plucked a twig from my hair and held it up pointedly.

"Then Prince Charming, he ain't." She snapped the twig in two and threw it aside. "Ash, he can't take his eyes off Laura whenever she's with Jackson. You can't tell me you haven't noticed."

"Why can't you just let me enjoy this?" I seethed at her. "We like each other. What's the big deal?" I wasn't totally clueless—it wasn't like I'd never wondered how much my transformation had to do with Seth's sudden courage. Or how much Laura's sudden dating had to do with it. But so what? I couldn't expect everything to change overnight even if I had.

"He doesn't even know you," Mouse shouted. "He didn't even know your mother died or that your dad's engaged. He's a jerk."

"You don't know what he's like when we're alone. He likes me. And I like him."

Mouse rolled her eyes.

"You like his butt. Big difference." She bit her lip. "You're changing for him. I can't believe you'd do that for a guy. I hardly recognize you anymore. You're all…pastel."

"It's more complicated than you think," I said, stung. I couldn't believe she'd say something like that to me. I was *not* changing for a guy. At least not the way she thought I was. She hadn't seen my dad's face when he asked me to be his best man.

"Ash, you're wearing a blouse. With *flowers* on it. You're going mainstream on me."

"So what? I think you're jealous." I knew that wasn't true, but I just wanted her to stop talking to me. I was afraid I'd spill my guts, and once I said everything out loud I'd know that what I was doing was stupid. I didn't want it to be stupid. It was working, wasn't it?

"Jealous of you and Seth? Please, I have a little self-respect."

"Of course, because you always know better than everyone else. You're always right."

"Are you tripping?" She gaped at me. "Are you having like some kind of psychotic episode? God, Ash." She turned on her heel and stalked away, gravel crunching under her granny boots.

I didn't stay to watch her go.

The next day, Mouse and I didn't talk to each other. I spent my spare working on the rest of my project. It was really coming along; the masks were taking shape. All that was left were the crowns, and then I could grout the mosaic and clean it off in the morning. I was still finding little bits of tiles and glass on the ground though. Every day I had to redo another portion, always different. But at least nothing else was breaking.

I was still trying to figure it out when Seth came up behind me.

"Hey, gorgeous," he said, kissing the back of my neck.

I smiled at him.

"Cool." He nodded at the mosaic briefly.

"Thanks. I've totally fallen in love with the whole thing, you know? Did you know in ancient Rome they—"

"Hey, Ash?"

"Yeah?" I guess he didn't really want to hear about ancient Rome or grouting techniques.

"Wanna go to the dance with me tomorrow night?"

I grinned. "Yeah."

"Cool." He nodded and strolled off, hands in his pockets.

I had a date for the dance. But no dress. I'd have to figure something out. Still grinning, I went to the girls' washroom to wipe off my hands. Mouse was there, smacking the tampon dispenser with the heel of her shoe. She stopped when the door opened. "Oh," she said. "Hi."

I nodded. I felt awkward, weird. I could tell she felt it too.

"Stupid machine's broken," she muttered. "It's always broken."

She looked like she wanted to say something else. Instead she put on her shoe and turned to leave.

"Seth asked me to the dance," I blurted out. Part of me wanted to prove to her that all the changes I'd made were working. Part of me wanted to prove it to myself as well.

"Good for you," she said blandly. "Some first boyfriend."

"Mouse, shut up."

After she left, one of the stall doors swung open. Laura

stepped out, glaring. I stifled a sigh. Great.

"You're going to the dance with Seth?" she asked coldly, washing her hands.

"Yes, I am," I answered over the sound of the running water.

The taps snapped off. "And now you think Seth's your boyfriend? God, that's pathetic."

I flushed.

"You don't actually think Seth's serious about you, do you?" She stepped right up to me, invading my personal space. The tip of her nose practically touched mine. The old Ash would have given serious thought to biting it.

"Back off, Laura," I said quietly.

"Or what?" She laughed. "You can bleach your hair and get new clothes, but you'll never be his type. Seth loves me. He always has. He knows it; I know it; we all know it."

She shoved me. I didn't shove her back. I stared at the mirror behind Laura's head. It cracked with a bang. She jumped, startled. I'd wanted it to crack and it had, exactly as I'd imagined it. I took a deep breath. I felt good, better than I had in a long time.

"Oh, my God," Laura said. She grabbed her purse and ran out of the bathroom.

I was left alone with the broken mirror, reflecting a hundred versions of myself in tiny sharp pieces. But which one was really me?

We learned in history class that the hearth used to be the centre of the house, where the pioneers baked their bread, and cooked their stew and warmed their bones when winter howled at the window. It was also where the old bards would sit and tell their tales, where women would spin wool, where magic was made. For some reason I think about that a lot.

I'm loving our fireplace now. It's not just a hole in the wall full of dust and soot. It's not even just where we used to sit on Christmas Eve to open all our presents.

It's something else entirely.

It's art and beauty and fire.

It's something I'm making all by myself, out of ashes.

CHAPTER 8

The next night I was elected babysitter. Katie was about as thrilled as I was.

"I don't want her to babysit," she sulked.

"Katie," Ella warned.

Katie pouted, ignoring me when I went into the kitchen to put on the kettle for tea. I could still hear them talking.

"Mom, I'm thirteen now. I don't need a *babysitter.*"

"I know, honey. But with that ankle, I don't want you alone all night."

"Well then why can't Julia stay with me?"

"Julia has a date with David," Ella explained.

"But, Mom…"

I had the urge to stick my fingers in my ears to block out the whining. She sounded like a small vexed poodle.

"It'll be fine. Be good."

"I'm always good."

I snorted to myself.

The door shut behind Ella, and the house was silent. Katie came into the kitchen and stared at me. I ignored her for a few minutes before looking up.

"You never have dates," Katie said.

I looked at her, one eye narrowed to a slit. "Shut up."

"Well, you don't. You don't even have a boyfriend."

"I said shut up, brat. Besides, I have a date, with Seth, for the big dance. So there."

"I'm hungry," Katie said, barely limping as she pushed passed me to the den. She threw herself on the couch. "I want a sandwich."

"You are not hungry. You just had dinner." I glared. "And three chocolate bars!"

"Did not!"

"I found the wrappers in my garbage, brat."

"They weren't mine," she said, pouting. But when the kettle whistled, she changed tactics. "Then I want a hot chocolate."

I muttered under my breath but made her one after I'd put a tea bag in the pot to steep. I put her cocoa very carefully down on the coffee table. I wasn't going to be accused of hurling cups at her again. Even though I was sorely tempted. But the new Ash just kept quiet and out of the way. The new Ash was getting on my nerves. But people seemed to like her more than the old Ash. And by people, I meant everybody except for Mouse.

Katie pulled at her chewing gum. "I'm bored."

I didn't say anything, just knelt in front of the fireplace. There were blobs of dried grout on my overalls. I went back to gluing the pieces of an old broken white cup I'd found in the garage onto the sides of the mantelpiece.

"I'm *bored*," Katie repeated.

"So go IM somebody."

"Put in a movie for me."

I didn't even look at her. "Put it in yourself."

"I'm *injured*," she said. "Remember? You did it to me."

"I did not hurt you," I said between my teeth.

She got up and went over to the cabinet, popping in a movie. The opening music to *Ever After* filled the room. She didn't limp at all. I narrowed my eyes at her.

"You little fake," I said. "You are so busted."

"Nu-uh. It still hurts a little."

"Please."

"Go ahead and tell them. Like they'd believe you." Katie flopped back down on the couch. She was right, that was the worst of it. It hadn't been long enough since I'd turned over a new leaf, to quote my proud father. Besides, he hadn't believed me the first time.

I left Katie watching the movie and went to my room. I'd already finished my homework. I wasn't in the mood to watch television. Instead, I went into Julia and Katie's bedroom. I wanted to see the dresses Julia had. Maybe I could borrow one for the dance.

On Julia's bed, the sheets were neatly tucked in, the quilt navy blue with white stripes. Katie's side was a mess of nail polish, magazines and old stuffed animals she wasn't quite ready to outgrow. Julia's side was as tidy as her bed, her desk uncluttered, and even her magazines had their own basket on the floor. I opened her closet door. Her clothes hung side by side. There were so many dresses I didn't know where to begin. Her shoes were lined up in a row, and none of them were scuffed.

I reached down to pick up a pair and my finger grazed what felt like a box. When I pulled it out I saw it was one of those cardboard boxes you can get at the grocery store. It was filled with food. There were bags of chips and boxes of cookies and even little shrink-wrapped moon pies. There were as many empty wrappers as full ones.

I went back to my room and sat on the edge of my bed, frowning. So Julia liked junk food. Who didn't? Why bother hiding it? I thought of her crying on the bathroom floor in the middle of the night and the way she was always brushing her teeth and the wrappers hidden in my garbage can.

I don't know how long I sat there until a knock at the door distracted me. I went to the front door and looked through the peephole. Seth grinned at me from the stoop.

I opened the door.

"What are you doing here so late?" I said, smiling.

"You said you were babysitting. Can I come in?"

"Sure." I stepped aside and let him in even though I knew my dad would have several different types of heart attacks if he knew. Especially when Seth and I ended up on the couch, stretched out with my overalls straps undone and my tank top pushed up so that my stomach was bare. His hand was warm over my bellybutton. We kissed for so long that I was finding it hard to catch my breath. All I could see was his smile and his dark brown eyes and all I could smell was his skin—soap and grass and aftershave. I couldn't believe he was here with me, whispering my name.

Seth Riley, pretty much lusted after by every girl in our high school, was sprawled across my couch. Correction: was sprawled across me, across my couch.

He slipped his hand farther up my tank top. I pulled away.

"Seth?"

"Mmm?"

"What's up with you and Laura?"

He froze. "What?"

"You just seem a little more…interested in her since she hooked up with Jackson," I continued.

He shrugged. "She's just my ex."

"Are you jealous?" I asked.

"I don't want to talk about her," he murmured over my lips. "Besides, I'm taking you to the dance, aren't I? Not her."

"Because I've changed?" I asked quietly. His only reply was a shrug. His mouth grew a little more persuasive.

"Ash, you're so pretty."

I snorted. I couldn't help myself.

"What a line," I teased.

His expression grew wary.

"What?"

I rolled my eyes.

"Well, come on," I wanted him to smile back, to share the joke with me and break the tension.

He didn't. His arms were strong under my fingers and his hair tickled my skin when it fell over his forehead. His tongue met mine. His hands got a little bolder. It wasn't easy to forget he was the wild boy and used to girls falling over themselves around him. And I hated that I was one of them.

But I couldn't help myself.

I grabbed his wrist though, before he reached the folded-down edge of my overalls.

"Seth, my dad could be home any minute."

"We'll hear him drive up."

I stared at him evenly. He might make me feel like I was a beeswax candle, melting under his flame, but I wasn't an idiot. Why did I have to keep reminding myself of that fact when he was around? Maybe I really was an idiot.

"Seth."

He sat up. "Yeah, okay."

I touched his shoulder. "Don't be mad." I probably should have booted his ass out of the house for sulking. I really didn't want to be replaced by some older girl who would put out without a fuss. Things were going so well. We just needed boundaries.

"I'm not mad," he said, "but maybe you're too young for me."

"What?"

He kissed my nose. "I'm just used to older girls."

My eyes narrowed. "I'm only a year younger than you."

"Maybe," he said. But he didn't look convinced.

"Don't be an ass, Seth. I just don't want to get caught on my dad's sofa."

He looked at me, clearly considering options that made my stomach flutter, before flashing one of his lopsided grins. My heart tumbled a little in my chest. See? Boundaries.

We kissed some more until I kind of wanted to tell him about the glass, and that I'd finally figured out what caused the worst of it. And how maybe, just maybe, I could figure out how to control it. I could be myself again.

"Seth." I drew away. "Can I tell you something?"

He pulled me close and kissed my jaw, my neck. "Sure," he said, clearly not listening.

"Seth—" I tried again, but then his mouth covered mine and his tongue touched mine and I kind of forgot what I'd wanted to say.

We kissed for a really long time. I barely heard the front door swing open. We leaped apart at the sound of someone clearing their throat. It was Julia.

"You scared the hell out of me!" I hissed, sitting up and struggling with my straps.

"Sorry." She gave Seth a considering look. "Hi, Seth."

He looked like he might be blushing, but he was grinning too.

"Hey. I guess I should go." He grabbed his coat and left. The front door slammed shut.

"He and Laura went out for like three years. They're always breaking up." Julia paused meaningfully. "And getting back together again."

"Not this time." I folded my arms.

Julia shook her head. "I think you should be careful. He always dates someone in between getting back together with Laura." She ran a hand through her hair. "I'm only trying to help, Ash…"

I cut her off before she could finish.

"Julia, I know what you're doing," I said. "I found the box in your closet."

I hadn't even really thought about what I was saying. I still thought maybe there was a really rational explanation. Her reaction said differently.

She paled. "What? I don't know what you're talking about."

I shook my head. A car door slammed, and then another.

"Yeah, you do."

"Please don't tell my mom," she whispered.

We just stared mutely at each other as the key turned in the lock and our parents stepped into the hallway.

I thought about talking to Dad about Julia the next morning, but he was late for work. He was already mad because I'd accidentally let a tiny glob of grout dry on the hardwood floor. You could barely see it. I even considered telling Ella at breakfast, but Julia looked so miserable. She ate all her pancakes and didn't stop by the bathroom, not even for a minute, before going out to the car. And I knew, because I was watching her. Maybe now that she knew I found her stash, she wouldn't make herself sick anymore.

I was pretty sure she would have driven off, but Ella

reminded her to wait for me because it was too wet out to walk. The silence in the car was thick as butter, smearing over everything I wanted to say.

"Julia."

She faked a smile, turned the radio on and cranked up the volume.

"Oh, I love this song, don't you?"

It was the first time I'd ever seen her speed, and I wouldn't have been surprised to hear the tires screech. She bulleted into a parking spot and then stopped so suddenly I jerked against the seat belt.

"Julia, seriously…"

She jumped out of the car, slamming her door.

"I don't want to talk about it."

She stormed away. I was really glad we were in separate grades and didn't see each other all morning. Just before lunch, Laura and Michelle leaned against their lockers, watching me smugly as I passed them.

"And the mirror *broke* when she looked at it," Laura smirked. "She's that ugly."

Noah and some guy I didn't know laughed. I was really glad Seth wasn't around. Ms. Harding stopped me in the hallway as I was stalking off.

"Ash, I just wanted to tell you the mosaic looks great." She was wearing silver earrings shaped like mermaids.

"Thanks," I said. I was glowing a little bit, like I did

when Seth kissed me the first time. I was really proud of my mosaic.

"I noticed there are a few cracked tiles in the queen's crown though."

The glow faded abruptly.

"Really?" I frowned. "Again?"

She nodded. "Easily fixed."

"Oh." I didn't know what to think. "Okay."

She smiled again, touching my shoulder. "You have a definite talent. Keep at it."

I didn't go by the panel at lunch even though I should have. I didn't want to see the sharp edges oddly broken. It didn't make sense. New Ash was just as much of a freak as old Ash. But at least old Ash got to speak her mind and be herself. I might as well have had laryngitis with all the talking I'd been doing lately. It didn't seem fair.

I skipped my afternoon classes so I could go to the mall and get a dress for the dance. I decided to go as a princess. Not a specific princess. Just a princess. I wished Mouse and I weren't fighting. She could have come with me. Although she would have protested everything. She would have gone into all of the name-brand shops and given lectures about sweatshops to all the customers.

I waited at the bus stop in front of the high school, hiding in the grimy shelter so no teachers would see me. I jumped when Seth poked his head in and grinned.

"You're skipping school."

I feigned surprise.

"I am? I thought I was going on a field trip. Malls can be very educational."

"They can be dangerous too," he said solemnly as the bus pulled up. "All that spilled ketchup in the food court. You could slip. I'd better come with you."

We sat in the back, and he held my hand.

Usually the mall stressed me out. It always had that slightly used smell, like the air had to be in too many places. At least today it was quiet. We stopped for iced lattes and made out by the escalator. Seth's hands were getting bold. I pinched him. Apparently, he had a lousy memory when it came to boundaries. When we went back to wandering, he paused in front of a window display. The mannequin had a blond bob and she was wearing a tiara and a pale pink dress that could only be described as frothy in the skirt and lacking in the top. It looked like a strawberry milkshake.

"You should get that one," Seth said.

I blinked, momentarily distracted.

"That one? Isn't it a little Pepto-Bismol?" I asked.

"You'd look good."

I glanced at it again, frowning. "Didn't Laura wear something like that last year for the big dance?" And the only reason I knew that was because her locker was next to mine and she'd torn a picture of her dress from a magazine and taped it inside the door. That, and the fact that she had talked about it to all her friends, ad nauseam, and loudly.

Seth shrugged. "Whatever. I just think it would look nice on you."

So I bought it.

And I even bought the matching tiara.

I got home an hour or so before dinner. My new dress was hanging over my arm in a garment bag. Dad and Ella were murmuring in the kitchen. Grimm was meowing at something under the couch.

I stopped when my father called my name.

"Where have you been?" he demanded.

It wasn't like I was late. It wasn't even five o'clock yet.

"I needed a dress for the dance tonight," I answered.

He was wearing a tie. He never wore a tie at home.

"Why are you dressed up?" I asked.

"I have to go to work, emergency meeting. I was supposed to leave half an hour ago."

"Oh. Bye."

"Your principal called," he said.

"He did?"

"You skipped class today, Ash."

"I needed a dress."

"You skipped class to go shopping? Without permission?" He shook his head.

"It's not like I had a test or anything."

"That's not the point."

"Dad, come on."

"Ash," he picked up his briefcase. "I really thought you'd stopped this sort of thing. You've been so good lately."

I deflated. "You mean I've been quiet and invisible." The glass fruit bowl on the counter shivered. I ignored it until it stopped.

"I just meant there've been no temper tantrums." He shook his head. "You can't skip class, Ash. You know that. Maybe you should stay home tonight."

I couldn't believe it. I'd been working so hard and now we were right back where we started. Well, maybe not entirely. I was mad and annoyed and hurt, but nothing exploded. The windows didn't so much as rattle.

"Dad, the dance is tonight!"

He looked briefly terrified. "Well, you should have thought about that before you skipped school." He kissed Ella and left.

I went to my room.

I cast a concerned eye on the glass frame over my mom's picture and the teacup on my dresser. They trembled, like there was a secret earthquake only they knew about. I breathed deeply and imagined silence. Steady dressers. Quiet teacups. The rattle faded. I let out the breath I hadn't realized I'd been holding.

I crawled into my closet to look for acceptable shoes, finding a pair of satin pumps my father bought me last year. I couldn't remember why.

I slipped into the dress and watched myself twirl in the mirror. I looked like a stranger, like any other sixteen-year-old girl on her way to dance with a cute boy. I wondered why that made me sad. I had what I wanted, didn't I?

I *was* going to the dance.

I stumbled on my third twirl, swearing loudly. I lifted the layers of chiffon. The right heel was broken, snapped clean off. I held the shoe in one hand and the heel in the other and cursed again, louder this time.

Now I was breaking everything? Not just glass? I took a deep breath. This was just a coincidence.

Ella knocked on the door.

"What?" I asked wearily.

She stood in the doorway. Her red hair fell down her back, and she was barefoot. She looked very serious. "I think you should go to the dance."

I couldn't believe what I was hearing. "Thanks," I said, stunned. "But…my shoes. The heel broke off."

"Oh," said Ella, taking a step into my room. "It's happened to the best of us." She took the shoe, fit the heel back where it was meant to be. "A little Krazy Glue will fix this right up."

I looked at her. "You think?"

"Sure," she nodded. "That's a pretty dress. Your old hair would have matched it perfectly," she added before leaving to find some glue. I just sat in my room and looked at my reflection. Ella came back ten minutes later with the shoe glued back together. She left it on the bed and didn't say anything else. It seemed so simple, a little glue and the pieces fit back together perfectly.

"Thanks. And, Ella…"

"Yes?"

"I never threw anything at Katie."

She looked at me steadily. I didn't flinch, just looked back. She nodded once, slowly.

"Okay." She didn't say anything else, just turned and left.

Julia came to the bathroom doorway, wearing a fairy-tale dress with a green plastic ball sewed onto the side.

"What are you supposed to be?" I asked.

She grinned. "The Princess and the Pea."

"Is David coming in a green suit?"

She snapped her fingers. "Wish I'd thought of that! Are you going with Seth?"

"Yes." My shoes pinched. I had to force myself not to kick them off. Instead, I tossed my hair back. If she could give me well-meaning lectures about the evils of certain boys, I could lecture her right back. And this time she was going to listen.

"Julia, you have to tell your mom."

She paled. "What? No. I told you, I'm fine."

I looked at her steadily. "Willingly throwing up a box of cookies is not fine. It's gross and a waste of good cookies."

"I had the flu."

"Give me a break, Julia," I said, but I said it gently. She looked terrified, like she was going to bolt.

"You don't know what you're talking about. You hate that we live here so you're making stuff up."

"I don't really hate that you're living here anymore." I pushed my hand through my hair. "But that's not the point. Look, I don't know, okay? I'm getting used to it. I guess your mom really does make my dad happy, and she's not so bad, but that's not the point. The point is you need help. You're not perfect."

The words seemed to echo and swell like a glass bubble forming at the end of a heated pipe. But this time, I didn't want the glass to break.

"I know I'm not perfect, damn it!" Julia all but shrieked. She slammed the door behind her as she left the room.

I stared at the door for a minute before following her. She was sitting on the edge of her bed, crying. Her fists were clenched.

"I'm not perfect, and I'm sick of everyone expecting me to be perfect," Julia said. "You can be as bitchy as you like, and no one cares."

"Oh boo-hoo," I said. "Everyone thinks you're great. My own father doesn't notice me unless I *do* act like a bitch. And now that I'm all quiet and wearing beige freaking pantyhose he loves me again."

"Do you know what I've heard for the past five years?" Julia yelled. "All I've heard is how I'm such a good girl and so helpful. Since my dad died, I had to keep being such an extra-good girl and not make extra trouble for my mother."

We were yelling at each other, and the really weird part was that it didn't feel like a fight. It felt really good not to just smile politely and nod my head. It felt like I'd been wearing a corset and it had just been loosened. I could breathe again.

There was a strangled sound from the door. We both turned sharply to see Ella, her eyes huge. Her hand was pressed to her chest.

"I never said that to you, did I?" Ella looked like she was going to cry too. I felt like an intruder and started to ease back toward the bathroom.

Julia deflated. "Ash never had to be a perfect little girl."

I gaped. I knew that tone. Julia was jealous? Of me? I didn't quite know how to process that.

"Yes I did," I said quietly. "Just not for as long as you did.

Everyone likes you," I added, confused. She wasn't perfect. I wasn't the only one who was a little broken, a little chipped.

She made a face. "I don't like me."

"Oh, honey." Ella sat next to her and stroked her hair.

"Tell her," I said softly.

Ella looked at me and then at Julia's wan face.

"Tell me what?"

"Ash."

"Julia." I mimicked her tone. I walked over to the open closet and yanked out the box of food and wrappers. Ella looked confused.

"You're hiding food?"

"Ask her what else she's hiding."

"Ash!"

I swallowed. Julia looked mad, but I knew I had to say it.

"Julia. Tell her."

Julia just closed her eyes, her shoulders slumping. When she spoke her voice was so soft we had to strain to hear her.

"She's right, Mom. I eat all this stuff at night when everyone's asleep, and then I...I..." She looked helpless. "Well, you know."

Ella frowned. "What are you trying to say?"

"I...throw it up."

"What?" Ella gasped. "What?"

Julia's voice was tiny now, like a seed. "It's true, Mom."

I backed out the door. Ella was holding onto Julia like

she wasn't ever going to let go. It made me miss my mom even more.

"Ash," Ella said as I was slipping out.

I looked up. "Yeah?"

"Thank you."

It felt kind of weird to be going to a dance after the day I'd just had. I put on my tiara and paced in the front hall, waiting for Seth to ring the doorbell. Katie was sitting in the living room, talking on the phone. She hung up, gaping at me.

"You look like a girl."

I snorted.

"I've always been a girl. Pink doesn't make me a girl."

"You didn't clean up my room today."

"I'm not cleaning your room anymore."

She pouted.

"Yes, you are." She wiggled her foot at me. I just arched an eyebrow.

"Forget it, brat."

There was a knock at the door, saving me from the rest of the conversation. I swung the door open. Seth stood there, smiling. The white of his Prince Charming shirt brought out his dark hair and intense eyes. He wasn't wearing tights, like all the princes in the old movies, just dark pants and boots. "Ready?"

"Sure. Let me get my jacket." All I had was my regular jean jacket. It would have to do. Ella came out of Julia's room and down the hallway.

"Have fun, you two."

"Thanks." I flipped my hair out from under my jacket collar. Katie cleared her throat repeatedly. I sighed. "Seth, this is Ella, and that's Katie."

Katie giggled. "Hi, Seth."

"Hello, Seth," Ella murmured. "Don't be home too late."

"Okay."

"And don't forget you promised to help me clean my room," Katie called out.

I looked at the vase of white lilies on the table beside the couch. It was near Katie's elbow. I stared at the vase, picturing it wobbling slightly, then tilting.

Nothing.

I stared harder. I knew I could do this. I just had to find my calm centre. I couldn't allow myself to get all bruised and shaken by every thought and emotion. And I couldn't repress everything until it just burst out of me. I imagined the thick gooey grout, smearing it with a paste knife, setting the tiny glass pieces in just the right order, building the vase up out of nothing, then wiping the grout away so nothing held it together.

The crack began as thin as a spider's web, but I knew it was there. The vase wobbled slightly, tilted, then broke with a crash. Green-tinged water spilled over the side table. Katie squealed and leaped to her feet.

Ella stared at the broken vase, then at Katie, who was standing on both of her feet. Too late, Katie shifted her weight back onto her uninjured ankle.

Ella's lips pursed. "Katherine Anne Wilson."

I smiled all the way to school.

The auditorium looked kind of nice, and it didn't smell like hot dogs, like the last dance when they had to use the cafeteria. The glitter-coated blue stars we'd cut out twirled overhead, and there were leaves in the corners and a stack of fat pumpkins. White steam billowed from the dry-ice machine. The music was loud and the strobe lights erratic. It was like every other school dance, only everyone was in costume.

Sleeping Beauty had apparently been cloned as she slumbered. There were easily a half-dozen of her. Sophie wore a long braided blond wig as Rapunzel. I saw Goldilocks, Snow White and a Beast in a furry mask. Mouse wore her Anne Boleyn dress with a red ribbon around her throat. I didn't go over to say hi.

Nicholas tapped me on the shoulder. He was dressed as

a pirate. "Mouse made me," he explained, when I lifted an eyebrow.

When I didn't smile, he asked, "So you and Mouse aren't talking?"

"I guess."

"Why?"

"It's complicated, Nicholas."

He looked irritated. "It isn't. She was trying to be your friend," he said, before losing himself in the crowd.

Seth took my hand and led me toward his friends. They were all dressed like fairy-tale princes, interchangeable with all the other fairy-tale princes.

Along one of the walls, across from a table piled with drinks and desserts, was the wooden panel, tiles glittering. I smiled.

"Seth, come see my mosaic."

He grimaced. "Art's not really my thing," he said, his breath warm in my ear. "I'll wait here."

"But don't you want to see what I made?"

"Sure. I see it all the time. Looks good."

He pulled on my hand, leading us onto the dance floor. Glitter shook free from the stars and fell around us like ice. His arms felt safe around me. His neck smelled like something green, like summer. The other dancers flailed around us, but he held me close. It was nice.

But I was still annoyed. And worse, bored.

Seth didn't notice. He was too busy trying not to be obvious about the fact that he kept looking at Laura dancing close to Jackson. It was really starting to piss me off. I was at a dance with the cutest boy I'd ever seen, and I was wearing a dress that was supposed to be pretty. Shouldn't I be feeling a lot happier?

I felt odd in my glued shoes, like I wasn't really there. My shoulders and back were bare in the dress. Seth's palm moved over my skin. Instead of enjoying the feeling, I kept thinking of how I wished Mouse and I were talking.

He held me, turning me with the music. My ankle twisted, and the glued heel snapped again. My foot slipped out of the shoe and I stumbled. We eased off the dance floor, and Seth led me to the chairs lining one of the walls. I lifted my shoe and flicked at the broken heel. It wobbled like a loose tooth.

"Bummer," Seth said. He looked over his shoulder. "I'll get us something to drink. Be right back."

He was gone before I could tell him I wasn't thirsty. I slouched in my pretty pink dress. Being a wallflower when you wore ratty old clothes was way different than being a wallflower all dressed up. Old Ash had nothing in common with Seth. But I didn't think new Ash did either. Except both her and Seth were wimps.

I went and stood for a long time in front of the mosaic masks. It was the only place in the whole auditorium where

I felt really comfortable. Seth wouldn't bother looking for me. I hadn't expected him to. Still, it might have been nice. I had already started to walk away when I heard the panel creak open. I turned back in time to catch a glimpse of Laura's dress disappearing behind it. Then the panel started to wobble. I suddenly noticed that its hinges were hanging oddly. The panel wobbled again, and I realized someone was trying to push it over from behind. I shouted as the whole thing teetered and began to fall toward the ground.

Everything seemed to be happening in slow motion. I dropped my shoe, rushed forward to stop the panel and caught some of its weight on my shoulder. I grunted at the force. The panel swung and one corner struck the ground. Someone else grabbed the panel and pushed until it leaned against the wall. Ms. Harding. Her eyes were wide.

"Ash, are you okay?"

I nodded, trying to find my tongue. I thought I might have swallowed it. While we stared at each other, Mr. Batra, wearing a tie with pumpkins, climbed onto the stage. He launched into a speech about school spirit into a crackly microphone. Finally, he ripped open one of the envelopes in his hand.

"I'm fine," I croaked. "Did it break?" I was almost too afraid to look. I ran my hand over my mosaic gently and didn't breathe until I was sure it hadn't cracked into pieces. The hinges dangled above me, like broken earrings. My arms ached. But at least my mosaic wasn't broken.

Ms. Harding frowned. "The hinges were loose," she said disapprovingly. "We'll have to get the panel reinforced. That was really dangerous."

She walked away, shaking her head as Mr. Batra continued his announcement.

"Your Harvest King is…Seth Riley!"

There were wolf whistles and hooting. Seth grinned when a teacher put a plastic crown on his head, and then he leaped off the stage, showing off. I didn't really pay attention since Laura had snuck back in and was standing casually by the refreshment table nearby, smirking.

"And your Harvest Queen is…"

Laura's eyes flickered toward the stage.

"Julia Wilson!"

Clapping, more whistling. But Julia was at home with Ella, clearing bags of junk food from under her bed. David wasn't here either. She must have called him. Eventually, the whispers made it to the stage, and Mr. Batra announced that Julia was not there. Laura looked furious, like someone had just shoved a lemon up her nose, all sour and bitter.

Seth sauntered over to us. He didn't say anything for a moment, just looked at Laura, who looked at him.

"Where's Jackson?" he asked. It was close to a sneer. She just shrugged.

"Let's dance," he said to me.

"Didn't you just see what happened?" I asked, pointing at the panel.

The music was loud enough that he pointed to his ears and shrugged, the international signal for "I can't hear you."

Or "I'm not listening."

"Come on," he tugged my hand. I dug in my heels.

"Seth, I am *not* in the mood to dance."

Laura smiled, stepped closer.

"I'll dance with you, Seth."

That's when I noticed the weird bulge in her purse. Narrowing my eyes, I grabbed the sequined clutch bag before she could stop me.

"What the hell are you doing?" she yelled.

I dumped her purse out on the nearby snacks table: lipstick, wallet, keys, a pack of gum…and a screwdriver.

I looked up, hoping for some kind of reaction from Seth, but he was busy smiling at Laura, and I knew that smile well. It was always followed by a long slow kiss. He didn't notice the screwdriver or didn't care, was entirely focused on the way Laura was pressing against him.

I couldn't help myself. She could wreck my date, but wrecking my art was a different matter altogether.

On the drinks table behind Seth and Laura, the punch bowl was a mosaic of colour. Suddenly it cracked with a loud bang, shards of glass skittering across the floor like ice. Red juice arced through the air, sticky and sweet. Laura shrieked.

Punch soaked her dress and showered Seth too, staining his white pants and shirt. He spluttered. Everyone around us laughed, the sound swelling around us like cicadas on a hot summer night.

I could see it all clearly, like a movie playing in my head. And if I tried hard enough, I could probably even make it happen.

Seth ran his hand down Laura's arm, then around her waist. He'd completely forgotten I was even there.

I waited for more fury to rip through me, for all the glass cups and the glass plates and the glass windows to rattle and fly into tiny sharp pieces like angry insects. For the punch bowl to explode.

Nothing even gave a whisper of sound. Nothing moved.

I should have felt sad that Seth still didn't see me, but instead I was relieved. I didn't actually care what he thought of me anymore. It just wasn't worth it. And I was proud of myself. I could have shattered the bowl, but I chose not to.

Everything was clear, like glass. It was like my very own personal mosaic had finally made a pattern I could understand.

I kicked off my other shoe. I finally felt grounded; barefoot was normal, comfortable. High heels, not so much. And I felt better, more myself. Even though, or maybe because, I was a barefoot almost-scruffy-again girl in a land of chiffon princesses.

"Goodbye, Seth," I said, smiling a real smile for the first time in weeks.

He finally flicked me a glance.

"What? Oh, Ash."

I shook my head.

"You two deserve each other."

I turned my back on them and went straight for Mouse who was screaming, "Yes!" and pumping her fist in the air like a sports fan. It looked really weird in her Renaissance costume.

"I feel like an idiot in this dress," I told her.

Her smile was huge.

"You look like an idiot in that dress."

I laughed. I was suddenly giddy, wild. "I'm sorry I've been such a bitch."

Mouse grinned. "Yeah, you have been. But I guess I have been too. So I'm sorry too. Maybe I shouldn't have said anything about Seth."

"No," I said. "You were right."

"You were right about his butt though."

"Hey," Nicholas said in mock protest.

Mouse grabbed my hand and linked arms with him, pushing away from the wall. "Let's dance."

We followed her out into the crowd. She pursed her lips.

"You're going to let me help you dye your hair back later, right?"

"Definitely."

She squeezed my hand as the strobe lights began to flash. "Look."

The net holding the requisite bundle of cheesy balloons opened up over the dance floor. Yellow, orange and red balloons floated gently down. Small index-card sized pamphlets fluttered down as well, like bird wings.

I bent and picked one up, looking at Mouse's grin.

"You didn't."

She tried to look innocent.

"Who, me?"

All the pamphlets decried animal testing for cosmetics. It was the little photos that were really disturbing.

"Mouse, ew."

She tilted her chin up. "Do you have any idea how many bunnies had to die to make all the lipstick and eyeliner and hair spray in this room tonight?"

Someone picked up one of the pamphlets and shrieked.

"Batra will totally know it was you."

She shrugged. "But he won't be able to prove it."

I hugged her briefly. "Wanna be my date for my dad's wedding?"

She winked. "As long as it's not at some golf-course country club. Do you know how many pesticides they use?"

I grinned back, and we let the music take us, spinning and whirling like pottery shattering in the air.

I got home late and all the lights were out, except on the porch. I closed the door as quietly as I could and tiptoed down the hallway. I stopped though, tilting my head when my eye caught a dim light from the desk lamp in the den. I stepped in to see if my dad was just sitting there, waiting to ground me.

The room was empty except for the mosaic, nearly finished, gleaming in the warm light. I knelt down in front of the fireplace and reached for my tools. The final bluebird took shape under my hands, and I glued pieces of white tile around it. Then I rummaged in the glass bucket for one of the chips of beach glass Mom used to keep in a vase on the kitchen table. It became the bluebird's eye, watching over us.

I felt a sense of peace and wonder steal through me, as though something painful and difficult had eased away. I felt

EPILOGUE

my power like a tiny ember inside my body. But this time it wasn't a forest fire, and I wasn't scared. I could easily break something now. But I didn't want to.

I'd have to talk to Dad in the morning. I had been angry with him for letting me get lost in the shuffle. For accepting me only when I wasn't myself anymore. Maybe he would listen now, mostly because I wasn't going to let him ignore me. And I wasn't going to be anyone other than myself, not ever again, not for anyone.

I would definitely have to start a new project soon. I might make a space in the basement for a little studio.

I stood up. "It's finished," I said out loud, half in disbelief. The mantelpiece was all blue and yellow and white, complicated chaos brought into some strange order.

A mess made beautiful.

*Alyxandra Harvey-Fitzhenry
studied Creative Writing and
Literature at York University
and has had poetry published
in several magazines.
Her first YA novel,* Waking, *was published by Orca Books.*